FREEDOM SKIES

FREEDOM SKIES

DAVE JOHNSON

Cover art by Creative Covers
ISBN: 9781739132675

To Rachel Laurence. With her help I can fly higher than the clouds.

The Rebel Runaway Series

1, Freedom Skies

2, Troubled Skies

3, Escape to the Skies (to be published in 2024)

The Stuck Series

1, Stuck in Time.

2, Stuck 1595: An Elizabethan Adventure.

3, Stuck 1824: A London Tale.

4, Stuck 1855: Lucy Travels East.

5, Stuck 1966: No Time To Groove.

6, Stuck in the Land of the Pharaohs.

7, Stuck Between Two Lives.

All "Stuck" books are stand-alone stories

CHAPTER ONE

His name was Jake, but everyone called him Hooky because he had a hook fitted to his left wrist. He had lost his hand in an accident at work and instead of his superiors at Fotheringay's Steam Works showing any sympathy they told him that it wouldn't have happened if he hadn't been so nosey. The factory bosses cut his pay, partly because now he would be less efficient with only one hand but also because the factory had lost several production hours while they unjammed the machinery and cleared the mess.

'You are damned lucky to have a job at all!' growled his supervisor, Grimes, 'If it was up to me, I would have fired you!'

Jake was naturally inquisitive. It was true that he had

no business plunging his hand into the depths of the steam processing machine in a foolhardy attempt to investigate why it had ground to a halt; after all he was only a cleaner. He wasn't to know that, once he had wiggled a drive belt and dislodged the obstruction, the machine would kick in with such pent-up anger and force that he would have no time to withdraw his hand. Jake would never forget staring in disbelief at the stump where his hand used to be. For a second, he felt nothing, then excruciating pain, as fierce and searingly bright as if the sun had entered the room. Then all went dark.

When Jake regained consciousness, he was at home with his wrist wrapped in a bloodied bundle of bandages. He later discovered that the factory doctor had cauterised the wound with a steam-heated knife while he was out cold. If he hadn't done, Jake would surely have bled to death. Then Jake was left to recover or die. Molly Scratchit, his neighbour, had kept vigil by his bed. She had known Jake's mother and father who had died in an explosion at the steam plant five years previously. Jake had just turned fifteen and had already started work there as an apprentice cleaner. After the explosion Fotheringay permitted Jake to stay in the factory-owned, lodgings the family had shared. In the early years, Molly had provided food and solace after his parent's death. Now, after his accident, her care was needed again.

A year had passed, and now the pain was gone. Sometimes Jake experienced the sensation of still having a hand and needing to scratch a fearsome itch, but he knew that was just in his mind. He looked down at the crude iron hook fixed to his wrist which the factory had 'generously' provided while taking its cost from his wage. With it, he could carry buckets of water and steady a sweeping brush.

The hook was also useful for scraping out the greasy grime that accumulated under the machines.

Now Jake had a new focus for his inventive mind - to replace the hook with something more practical and aesthetically pleasing. Jake's mother would have been shocked to see his room. She had aspired to decorate it with damask wallpaper, like the ones she had seen in London's fancy houses when she worked as a maid. She was never able to afford more than a yearly coat of whitewash and Jake had not repainted the room since she died. Now, an intricate pattern of diagrams drawn in graphite covered the walls. Some were versions of plans Jake had memorised when cleaning the Design Room. One advantage of being a lowly cleaner was that if he worked as fast as he could in the machine rooms, it allowed him more time to study any plans left out in the Design Room after the engineers had all gone home. Sometimes Jake was able to scavenge paper from the bins and make notes. Occasionally, he would be delighted to find a partially completed diagram, perhaps spoiled by an inkblot, and he would carefully fold it up and hide it beneath his shirt.

Jake wasn't selective about what diagrams he reproduced on his walls, but if they had cogs and gears and were driven by clockwork, they had pride of place. He had taken apart his parents' bed and refashioned it into a desk which he positioned beneath the only window in the room, and it was here that he spent most of the hours when he was not at work. Jake spent his time designing fantastic machines, and most of his wages were spent getting items cast in the foundry. He felt fortunate because Old Nick at the foundry had been his father's drinking companion and rarely charged him full price for the work he did. Old Nick slipped Jake's projects in alongside other jobs when he had fired up the furnace. Occasionally Jake would buy Old Nick a pint or two in his favourite pub, The Rat and Whippet. Jake never drank alcohol himself and the water wasn't safe to drink, but he would nurse a glass of milk and listen to Old Nick's tales of life in The Rookery before the authorities walled it off from the rest of London.

Jake made his way through The Rookery, oblivious to the rats, which scurried through the sewage, dragging remnants of food from the gutters. The Rookery, a notorious slum in the St Giles area, was home to most of the workforce who ensured London was the world's richest and most powerful city. Men, women and children toiled in the factories that bordered the district, but The Rookery also harboured gangs of thieves and murderers who would slit your throat for the price of a bottle of beer. With a room to himself, Jake was one of the lucky ones. There were many boarding houses where up to forty people slept in one room.

Entering The Rookery was easy. No one questioned workers returning from a day's work, or even those from the upper echelons of society in search of a night's bawdy entertainment in the city's red-light district; it was getting out that was the problem. Residents had to show soldiers guarding the gate papers that proved they had good reason to leave The Rookery. Jake could never acquire such permission because a doorway in the slum district's walls led straight into Fotheringay's Steam Plant, so the authorities saw no reason why Jake should ever need to leave, but he had other ideas.

'Definitely not! I won't hear of it! Have you no shame?' hissed Arabella Fotheringay, keeping her voice low in case the servants could hear her. 'Remember who you are. You will bring disgrace to our family name. I don't know what has got into you. I blame Carrington for putting ideas into your head. I've always thought employing him was a bad idea. We only took him on as a favour to a friend of your father's who was in the Air-Fleet. Years spent floating about in a balloon have put air into his head, but I won't have him inflicting his demented ideas on you. I'll hear no more about it. The matter is closed!' Charlotte's mother stamped her foot and flounced out of the room.

Charlotte

I tried to walk calmly and serenely back to my room, but unfortunately, I completely failed and stumbled up the stairs. Mary, one of our maids, was waiting on the landing until I had passed, and she rushed to help me. She noticed the tears running down my cheek, so I made an excuse about getting a speck of dust in my eye, making it water. My eyes were stinging, and I realised my anger was beginning to burn fiercer, so now I'm pacing around my room, my sanctuary, trying to calm down. I can see on my bed my favourite china doll. She's wearing a dress that I made myself, and although at eighteen I'm too old to play with dolls, she still has pride of place in my room. Actually, I should say 'rooms' because I have a doorway that connects with the nursery. I still call it that, even though I've grown up and Nannie has long since left us. It was a sad day when my parents decided to 'let her go' because I was to have private tutors instead. I had spent every day with Nannie Susan for as long as I could remember. Even when we went to church every Sunday, I sat with her, not my parents. I suppose I have to be positive and think that at least another child benefited from her loving nature. I still feel guilty that I loved Nannie Susan much more than my mother or father. Words like duty and responsibility describe my relationship with them. I saw them occasionally for fleeting moments during the week, and of course, I was taken to the drawing room by Nannie Susan to say goodnight to Mother every evening; Papa always worked late.

As I open the door to the nursery, I try to picture my mother in these two rooms, but the memory evades me. I certainly doubt my father ever came here. Now I am an adult, you might expect me to use one of the reception rooms downstairs in my spare time, but I still prefer to be in the nursery. I can read and sew in this room. By the window stands my pride and joy, my Singer Sewing Machine. It was a gift from Papa. I imagine he was given it as an inducement to do business with the company up in Scotland that made it. No matter, I enjoy creating with it. Mother doesn't really approve. She thinks that embroidery would be a much more ladylike pastime for me, but being ladylike has never been one of my aspirations. Don't misunderstand me -I've been told I look very pretty in my ballgowns, I can play the piano quite well and sing too. I can dance, I know how to Waltz and Polka, so in my mother's eyes, I am perfectly equipped to join London society and find a wealthy husband. Oh! The thought of it. An endless round of balls, concerts and high teas, culminating in a betrothal to a dull, bigoted and self-important army officer. It's like a dark cloud hovering in the distance, waiting to engulf me.

Talking of clouds, I wonder if it's going to rain because I think I'll go out. How odd! As I'm checking the weather through the window, I see Carrington, our chauffeur, walking away from the house carrying a small case. He passes through the ornamental gates, glances back, and then vanishes. Oh, bother! I was going to ask him to take me to Papa's factory. Never mind. I can get a hansom cab instead. I wonder where dear old Carrington is going? Once Nannie Susan had left, Carrington took her place in my heart. There was one particular summer when I was fifteen and Carrington acted as my chaperone on several day trips. Father trusted him because he had a military background, and Mother was only too pleased not to have to come out with me. She hadn't yet arranged the succession of dull, simpering lady companions that were to arrive later in the year to accompany me to art galleries and concerts. Carrington has a sense of adventure about him. I remember the day he let me climb a huge tree, and when I got stuck and scared coming down, he just told me to pause, breathe deeply, and then go higher and find another way down. And I did! I was so pleased with myself. He told me not to tell my parents I had climbed a tree! One thing I do regret, though, was telling them about the day that he met an old friend from the Air-Fleet in Hyde Park. I couldn't believe it! This chap had a hot air balloon and was having a picnic, and before you knew it, we were all soaring up into the sky. It was the best day of my life, and I just had to share it with my mother and father, but to my surprise, they were both incredibly annoyed. Ever since that day, I've wanted to take to the skies, which is why I am so upset about Mother's refusal to let me join the Air-Fleet. This calls for a rearguard action. I'm going to see Papa at work and try to persuade him before Mother gets to speak to him. I'll put on a dress that I know he likes, the green one with the ribbons and bows, too frilly for my taste, but it should help me get him on my side. I wonder if I would have to jump through all these hoops if I was a boy! I remember the day when I asked my father if there were any women running factories like his, and he just laughed and laughed at the idea of it. I tried not to let it show, but that really hurt me.

'What is so wrong with wanting to join the Air-Fleet?' muttered Charlotte as she left the house, 'Just because there aren't currently any women pilots, it doesn't mean there should be none in the future!'

Jake was far from being a ladies-man. With his disfigured hand and lowly status, he knew he was hardly a good catch. What's more, he lacked the charm and ease that others his age had when chatting with the fairer sex. He had seen girls' eyes glaze over when he tried to talk about the things that inspired him; cogs, gears, and machinery. They wanted someone who would make them laugh, wine and dine them and could one day earn enough money to support a family. Jake could promise none of those things.

'Hello, Maggie,' said Jake. Maggie was different. 'Let me take that basket. 'Did you make a good batch of candles? I bet the walls in your house are dripping with wax,' he laughed. They had struck up something less of a friendship than a mutually advantageous arrangement.

'Mustn't grumble,' she replied, 'I thought we would visit Camden. It's getting quite respectable around there.' Jake stood to one side, trying not to attract attention whilst Maggie flirted with the guards on duty at The Rookery gates.

'I'm glad you are on duty Bert; you are much more handsome than that other one with the big nose.'

'Ere, I'll tell 'im that!'

Don't you dare! Here's my hawker's certificate if you want to check it.'

'No, you're alright, Maggie, we know you.'

Maggie passed through the gates daily, and so too, on occasions, did Jake. It was a small price to pay, carrying her basket for an hour or two, as she called at the servants' entrance of houses belonging to middle-class Londoners, trying to sell her wares.

'Do you reckon you'll ever get a permit to visit Toff Town?' asked Jake. He was referring to the exclusive area bordering Hyde Park, nicknamed Toff Town by the working classes. Like The Rookery, it was a gated community, but there the similarity ended.

'No, I don't even bother trying. I know all the rich and important people live in the villas and mansions there, but I don't reckon they would want my homemade candles. A bit too wonky for them. Even the servants would turn their noses up at them. I'm best sticking to my regular customers!'

'Just as well,' laughed Jake, 'Some of those houses are so big we would end up walking twice as far just to get from one to the next.'

'There's a lot of people in The Rookery who would love to get into Toff Town. They would come back with a sack full of jewellery, watches and gold candlesticks,' commented Maggie.

'Nothing in Toff Town for me,' replied Jake. 'As usual, I'm searching for something much more valuable.'

'And what's that then? As if I didn't know where you will be going after we've finished in Camden.'

'Yes, I'll be off to Great Russell Street to visit the British Library Reading Room, and what's more valuable than all the gold and diamonds you can carry?' Maggie laughed; she knew what was coming as it was a phrase he often repeated and she joined in with him:

'Knowledge, my dear, knowledge!'

'I 'ope yer not in a fearful hurry, Miss,' said the cab driver apologetically, 'Only my 'orse is a bit under the wevver. We will get there, Miss; only we might take a little longer than usual.' Charlotte reassured him that he could take his time, and the driver continued. 'It's a funny thing, but the roads ain't half as busy as usual. Generally, at this time, I would be stuck behind the Household Cavalry, taking up all the road as though they owned it and looking down their noses at the likes of me, but I ain't seen hide nor hair of em.' Charlotte smiled sympathetically, not knowing if he was complaining or not and, refusing his offer of help, she climbed into the cab and shut the door. The driver hoisted himself onto his seat behind the cab. Thankfully he didn't try to continue chatting through the hatch in the roof, allowing Charlotte time to prepare what she intended to say to her father.

The two girls looked down at the unconscious figure lying at the foot of the steps of number 74 Granby Terrace, more commonly known as Madame Boo-Boo's. It wasn't one of the more popular brothels in The Rookery, but it was very convenient for The Rat and Whippet.

'Looks like he was too drunk to get indoors this time,' laughed Sadie. 'I'll bring him a cup of tea if we ain't busy with breakfast quickies.'

The man sprawled on the pavement was Oliver Moon. Woe betide any one who found themselves unconscious on the streets of The Rookery. They would wake up minus their purse and most of their clothing, but this man was different. He was no stranger. Depending on his mood, he would offer those he met a drink or a fight, or sometimes both. Oliver always won, for he was no street brawler; he had been that rare type of army officer who enjoyed being at the forefront of the battle. Oliver was trained and dangerous, but his "hellraiser" tendencies and disregard for authority meant that throughout his career he was continually moved sideways, from regiment to regiment, until eventually, he lost his commission. Oliver's long leather coat, white silk scarf and goggles indicated that he had once been a member of the Air-Fleet, and, despite the petty thieves that roamed the streets at all hours, Oliver's clothes were quite safe; his top hat, which had come to rest a few feet from where he lay, would wander no further.

As Charlotte climbed the steps to her father's factory, she was surprised to see a face she recognised. It was Pip, a young servant from the Fotheringay household, who rushed past her. Pip was in too much of a hurry to notice her, but the stocky man in the long black coat standing guard at the entrance to the Steam Works wasn't.

'Morning, Miss Fotheringay,' he said, tipping his hat. It was Hastings. Charlotte did not care for him. He and his five subordinates answered directly to her father and provided effective policing throughout the factory simply by instilling fear into the workforce. She had heard rumours that Hastings was violent and a bully. The rumours were true; one day, a machinist had suggested that the workforce should have rights such as safer working conditions and shorter hours. It took that worker a full two hours to crawl home from work later that day after a short encounter with Hastings, and a further two weeks for his broken ribs to heal enough to return to work. That broken man was a visual deterrent to anyone else with radical ideas. His family suffered too; they needed his wages to survive and were left with debts to moneylenders.

Charlotte nodded an acknowledgement and hurried to her father's office. She knocked and went in without waiting for a reply. At first, Charlotte struggled to see her father as she peered into the gloomy room through the fug of cigar smoke. Brown was the predominant colour in the office which had dark, oak-panelled walls and drab linoleum. Dominating the room was a massive mahogany desk behind which sat Leonard Fotheringay. He looked up from his papers, surprised by the sudden intrusion of his daughter.

'Charlotte, my dear, this is a surprise. It's always a delight to see you, but you don't usually come unannounced.'

'I simply couldn't wait, Papa. I want to talk to you about my future.'

'Oh dear,' sighed Fotheringay, 'I was worried that might be why you are here. Your mother is quite upset.' Charlotte's heart sank. She had hoped to circumvent her mother.

'Oh! She has been in contact with you?'

'Yes, a servant brought a letter,' he waved a piece of paper, then replaced it on his desk. 'I've only just read it.'

'But surely you see, Papa, that it would be perfectly acceptable for me to join the Air-Fleet. Your social position will not be compromised. After all, it's 1860. Females should be represented everywhere: in the military, in industry and in the Government.'

'Honestly, child, I think you read far too many fairytales when you were young. It's time to put all this behind you. You must engage with the real world. Now, I have got good news for you. Major Drummond has been invited to dinner this evening. He's what I believe your mother would call a good catch. He's very well thought of in High Command.'

'Drummond!' exploded Charlotte, 'He's a pompous ass!'

'Now, now. That's no way for a lady to talk!'

'It's the truth!'

'You must apply yourself, Charlotte. Nothing will come your way without a little effort. I think it's time we got you home. Carrington will be here shortly and…Damnation! I forgot. The letter from your mother said she had to let him go. We'll have to make our own way home.'

'What? What do you mean?'

'Oh, we can get a hansom cab or a hackney carriage…'

'No, no!' interrupted Charlotte. What you said about Carrington!'

'Your mother has terminated his contract. You will find for yourself when you are running your own household that sometimes difficult decisions must be made.'

'But Carrington? What has he done to deserve being sacked?'

'We let him go,' corrected Fotheringay. 'Sometimes you have to cut out a diseased branch to protect the tree as a whole, and I fear the ideas he was feeding you, the nonsense about the Air-Fleet, is evidence that our household had been infected. I won't stand for it in this factory, and your mother won't tolerate it at home.' Charlotte struggled to take in the information and felt a combination of anger and guilt. It was her fault that a trusty servant had lost his job. It was too much to bear. Then Charlotte heard a loud bell ringing. Disorientated by the noise and feeling dizzy she stumbled out of the room and into the corridor, where she was swept along in the midst of hundreds of workers who had just finished their shift.

CHAPTER TWO

Jake

My hook is resting on the book to stop the pages from flipping over. Sometimes I forget I have a hook instead of a hand, but not right now. If it's possible for an inanimate object to taunt you, well, that's what it's doing. Maybe I should be grateful. If I hadn't had the accident, then I would have been like everyone else. Working, eating, and sleeping. I wouldn't have learned to read; I wouldn't spend all my time trying to solve mechanical engineering problems; I wouldn't be risking my liberty by sneaking into the British Library to read books about physics. So, is that a blessing or a curse? The hook is a physical reminder that I am less of a human than those around me, like something from a freak show.

Sometimes I despair, but then at other times, I'm fired up with determination to improve my situation. I want to create something that is not just a facsimile, a copy, but will be better than a normal hand - functional and efficient. I shake my head to try and clear away negative thoughts and convince myself that I'm just nervous that my design will be a failure. Then what would that make me? My hopes and aspirations don't reach any further into the future. I'm a factory cleaner, and every day Grimes, my supervisor, makes it clear that I should think myself fortunate to be employed at all. So I have to be diligent. I have to work harder than anyone else and not give him an excuse to get rid of me. I know full well that his brain is as much use as a head full of porridge, and should he ever recognise that I am cleverer than him, it would be to my disadvantage. He will make sure I never progress. I'll go down, not up!

Jake left The British Library Reading Room the same way he had entered . It was an institution that would not have permitted the likes of him to use the front door, so he stuffed his notes into his jacket, climbed out of a second-floor window onto a narrow ledge and closed the window from the outside. Jake wasn't unduly worried about finding the window locked in the future because he had loosened the screws that held the window catch so it could be easily prised open, but so far Jake had always found it as he had left it. He wasn't concerned about losing his balance either because running horizontally along the wall, just above his head, was an iron waste pipe, and the hook on his left hand fitted around it perfectly. Eventually, it connected with a downpipe, and again his hook was ideal for helping him descend the building. There was no risk of slipping due to tired fingers.

Jake would have liked to stay longer, but he had arranged to meet Old Nick to collect the latest piece cast in the Foundry. He was excited by what he had discovered in the library. He had been researching magnetism and was confident he could use its properties to power some of his inventions.

An hour later, Jake was in The Rookery. The tumbledown cottages and patched-up houses were in complete contrast to the elegant library in Bloomsbury that he had just left. Here, buildings had extra floors and extensions tacked on with little regard for the laws of physics. It was a wonder that some of them did not come crashing to the ground. Often a house only seemed to be held up by its neighbours - if one went, they all would!

Charlotte was also in The Rookery, although she was only just starting to realise it. She had been swept through the back entrance of the factory in a daze by the tired and dirty workers. Some needed their beds; others were searching for a pint of ale in a friendly pub. Now that the crowd had dispersed, Charlotte realised she was lost in what seemed to be a foreign country. The streets were narrow and lined with grime. Gangs of street urchins roamed aimlessly. She gasped as a bucketful of filthy water was thrown out of a window, narrowly missing her. She had to mind where she walked because the gutters were home to myriad festering, rotting substances that may once have been food. The rats didn't care; they grazed quite brazenly.

The air was filled with the sound of men shouting and babies crying. Charlotte chose to walk in the middle of the road away from the doorways, fearful of the men and women slumped there and, judging by the empty bottles surrounding them, who were feeling the effects of too much cheap gin. Charlotte realised that in The Rookery, there would be no friendly policeman to ask directions of and no possibility of finding a hansom cab; neither would dare venture into these parts. Nor could she retrace her steps through the warren of alleys and passageways. Panic rose and caught in the back of her throat.

'Now then, what have we here?' wheedled a voice behind her. Charlotte spun round to see a man in his twenties wearing a battered bowler hat decorated with a rook's feather tucked into a red band. His crooked smile revealed a mouth full of blackened teeth. 'On our holidays, are we? I can see by your fancy clothes and milky-white complexion that you don't come from these parts. Looking for an adventure, eh? You've come to the right man?' Charlotte shuddered; she had never felt so frightened before. The man reached for one of the ribbons on her sleeve, but Charlotte snatched her arm away. 'I see, so you like playing hard to get. I can play that game.' This time he clamped his hand around the top of her arm and pulled her roughly towards him. Charlotte was so shocked and frozen with fear that she could not utter a word or even make a sound.

'Unhand her immediately,' boomed someone from behind her. There was a familiarity to the voice which woke Charlotte from her trance, and she snatched her arm away and turned to face him.

'Carrington!' she gasped.

'Ma'am,' he replied, keeping his eyes on the man in the bowler hat who had drawn a knife and was now advancing in a menacing, crouching manner. 'I urge you to desist, Sir,' warned Carrington.

'Desist is it?' sneered the aggressor. 'I'll show you desist,' and he lunged forward, attempting to plunge the knife into Carrington's chest. For an older man, Carrington was surprisingly nimble. He stepped to one side and, as the ruffian's momentum took him past, Carrington smashed his fist down on the man's neck, sending him sprawling to the ground. Then, before he had time to recover, Carrington stamped his foot down with full force on the hand holding the knife. The man let out a yelp of pain and, not surprisingly, released his weapon. A kick from Carrington sent it skittering across the street, where a group of urchins, attracted by the fight, seized it and disappeared down a back alley. A well-aimed kick to the man's ribs drew another cry of pain. Carrington stepped back.

'I requested that you should desist. I now think it is time that you took your leave.' Scuttling away like a crab, the injured man scrambled to his feet and retreated down a dark passageway with his broken hand clutched under his armpit. A steady handclap sounded from across the street, where a man sitting on the ground and wearing a long leather coat, raised a teacup in salute.

'What are you doing here, Carrington?' asked Charlotte.

'It might be more apt if I were to ask you the very same thing, Miss, but to answer your question, now that the Fotheringay household no longer employs me, I have come to stay a while with my sister, who resides in this vicinity.'

'Oh, Carrington! I didn't mean to cause you so much trouble.'

'Might I suggest that we retire to my sister's house for a cup of tea, and then we can escort you out of this area?… Oh dear!' Four men were steadily approaching, all wearing bowler hats trimmed with feathers. Charlotte squealed in fright and backed behind Carrington.

'We was told that there was someone 'ere in need of bein' taught a lesson,' said one of the gang, pulling a cosh from beneath his coat.

'If you get a chance, Miss, make a run for it,'

whispered Carrington, 'I'll try to hold them off.'

'...An I reckon it's you,' continued the thug. Someone whistled. It was a jolly, cheerful tune that didn't seem to suit the circumstances but had the desired effect. Everyone turned their heads to see the intimidating figure of Oliver Moon slowly buttoning his leather coat.

'We was only having a bit of fun, Mr Moon,' said one of the louts, 'No offence. We were just going to leave anyways. C'mon, boys.' As they left, he muttered, 'We are going to have to do something about 'im.'

Meanwhile, Oliver was staring at Carrington. 'My God! Warrant Officer Carrington? From the Air-Fleet?'

'At your service, Sir, and much obliged for your intervention. I believe you are Group Captain Moon?'

'The very same.'

'Who were those ruffians?' asked Carrington.

'One of the local gangs,' replied Oliver, 'They are called The Black Feathers.' He bowed and held out a hand to Charlotte, who shook it demurely. 'Why don't we have a drink at The Rat to celebrate our renewed acquaintance.'

'No offence, Sir, but another time. I think Miss Charlotte has had quite enough excitement for one day. We shall go to my sister's house for a cup of tea.'

'Then I shall escort you there, after which, as I've already had tea, a glass of port back at the Rat will do nicely.'

Charlotte was silent for the short walk through the maze of streets and alleyways leading to Carrington's sister's house. Most of the talking came from Oliver, who seemed oblivious to the fact that he had witnessed a violent attack just moments before and reminisced about his time in the Air-Fleet. They arrived at their destination without further mishap, whereupon Oliver promptly wheeled around, and with a cheery wave, returned to the pub to chase away his morning demons. Carrington guided Charlotte through the doorway of his sister's house.

'Cissie, I would like to introduce you to Charlotte Fotheringay,' he said to the small, neat woman dressed in black who appeared in the hallway. 'Miss Charlotte, this is my sister, Cissie Newton. She has been kind enough to give me board until I get back on my feet again.'

'It's not much, just a few rooms, but it's all I can afford. We moved here when my husband, God rest his soul, was ill. Since then, my brother has been kind enough to send me money each week. That will stop, of course, now he doesn't have a job. The neighbourhood is not the most desirable, but I'm too old to worry about keeping up appearances.'

Charlotte's response was completely unexpected - she burst into tears. Carrington was flustered and had no idea how to respond. Cissie was puzzled; she had no idea why the daughter of her brother's ex-employer should be standing in her hallway, but she stepped forward and took her by the hand.

'Come child, let's sit down and have some tea.'

'I don't suppose there is somewhere I could lie down for a moment, is there?' stammered Charlotte between sobs, ' I feel a headache coming on. I need to lie down in a darkened room.'

'Of course! I only have two bedrooms. You shall have mine.'

Charlotte lay on the bed, knowing there was no possibility that she could fall asleep. Apart from the throbbing headache, there were her troubled thoughts whirling around. When she had expressed her ideas about joining the Air-Fleet, it was in search of an abstract concept

- the joy of sailing through the skies. She had never truly considered that, as the Air-Fleet was an arm of the military, violence and bloodshed might come her way. Now that she had experienced a fight for the first time, as brief as it was, she was racked with shame about how terrified and useless she had felt. Was she just a fraud?

'Damnation!' shouted Fotheringay angrily, reading the note a servant from home had just delivered. He banged his fist down on the table. There was a knock at the door. 'Come in,' he responded tetchily.

'You wanted to see me, Sir?' asked Hastings.

'I do, Hastings. This day is going from bad to worse! First, I hear that Major Drummond has cancelled his invitation to dinner because of something wrong with his stupid horse, and then I hear that my daughter has not returned home. Did you see where she went? Did she get a cab?'

'I'm sorry, Sir. I saw her arrive, but she definitely did not leave by the main entrance. I never left my post.'

'But where can she be?'

'Either she is still in the building, or she has left by the only other exit and is in The Rookery.'

'The Rookery! My God! Conduct a search of the building and if you do not locate her, lead a search party into The Rookery. Find her and bring her back using whatever means is necessary!'

Jake entered The Rat and Whippet in search of Old Nick. He found him seated on a bar stool beside a man wearing a long leather coat with goggles slung loosely around his neck. Jake recognised him.

'Milko, my old friend,' Oliver called out warmly. Jake smiled in return. The first time they had met, Oliver had tried to buy him a drink, then nearly taken offence at Jake's request for milk, but instead had burst out laughing and thereafter dubbed Jake' Milko'. It was better than being called 'Hooky', but Jake wished people would call him by his name. The only people who did, like Old Nick and Molly, were those who had known him since he was a boy.

Oliver ordered pints of ale for himself and Old Nick and milk for Jake. Just then, another man came through the door. Jake lowered his head and slid his hooked hand beneath his coat. He had no reason to hide but would rather go unnoticed, for he knew this man and did not like him. He was a bully called Banks, who worked for Hastings at the factory. Jake saw that Banks was carrying a club.

'I'm looking for a young girl of eighteen…' he announced to the pub.

'Oy, oy! Find one for me too!' shouted someone from the back of the room. Banks scowled at the man, slapping the club against his hand in a menacing fashion. The laughter that had erupted in response to the quip subsided.

'I said, I'm looking for a young lady. She must be lost and doesn't belong in The Rookery. She is wearing a green dress decorated with ribbons and bows. Has anyone seen her?' There was silence, apart from the sound of Oliver ordering another drink. He had downed the previous beer in one gulp. 'If anyone knows anything, you should report it to Fotheringay's,' continued Banks before leaving the pub.

'But first, you should report it to me!' shouted the comedian at the back of the room, 'I'll know what to do with her.' Once more, the pub erupted into coarse laughter. Oliver gazed thoughtfully into his beer.

'I suppose I'd better go and warn old Carrington,' he said. 'After this beer.'

'Cheer up, it may never happen!' laughed Old Nick, 'Why are you looking so glum, Jake.'

'Seeing someone from Fotheringay's is a painful reminder that I might never improve my circumstances. I feel like I'm wasting my life. I'm sure I've got potential, but I won't achieve it pushing a broom around the Steam Works.'

Oliver had almost finished his drink when the pub hushed. Three men wearing bowler hats decorated with rook's feathers shouldered through the door. The eldest man approached the bar. He wasn't a pretty sight! An ugly scar stretched from the corner of his mouth almost up to his left eye. His hair was long and silver, reaching past his collar. The landlord was about to serve another customer but abandoned him and approached this newcomer.

'Good afternoon Mr Jack, or is it evening now? What can I get for you?' said the landlord nervously.

'Two pints,' replied Crusty Jack. The landlord placed them on the bar; Crusty Jack slid one across to Oliver.

'Much obliged, Mr Jack,' nodded Oliver.

'A word, Mr Moon,' said Crusty Jack quietly. Oliver leaned in. 'It's time our little arrangement came to an end.' He clinked his glass against Oliver's. 'I just want to say no hard feelings; you've put a little business our way over the last year and I am very appreciative, but I can no longer afford you protection from my boys. There's been a bit of grumblin' amongst 'em. They are worried people will think they are soft, and that will never do. We ain't lookin' for trouble, but we ain't going to run away from it neither.' Oliver nodded and clinked his glass against Crusty Jack's. He understood. If he crossed the Black Feathers gang again, they would seek retribution.

Crusty Jack finished his drink quickly and left with his two companions. Oliver tapped the side of his glass with a fingernail, a wry smile on his face. The landlord looked up, thinking Oliver was trying to attract his attention. He wasn't, but he downed the rest of his beer and pushed his empty glass across the bar.

'Why not?' he said.

Oliver drank his next beer steadily. He wasn't unduly concerned about the change of affairs. What will be, will be. Then he realised he had meant to warn his old friend Carrington about the man asking questions. He muttered his goodbyes to Jake and Old Nick and lurched out of the pub feeling the effects of a large volume of beer drunk over a short period.

Old Nick smiled as he watched Oliver leave.

'He goes at it like a bull at a gate,' he laughed. 'I reckon Mr Moon has some inner horrors that he is trying to drown in beer.' Jake was more interested in the notes he had made during his visit to the Library.

'I found out some fascinating facts about magnetism today,' he said to Old Nick, 'And now that you've given me the last cog that I need to construct my new hand, this day is shaping up to be a day like no other.' Little did Jake know!

Coincidentally, Jake walked away from the pub in the same direction that Oliver Moon had a little while earlier, although, having drunk nothing stronger than a glass of milk, Jake's gait was very much steadier. As he emerged from Rutland Passage, Jake heard a commotion. He slowed his pace and advanced warily. Jake always avoided confrontation, but there really was no other way for him to get home than to follow this route. As he had suspected, there was a fight in progress. A circle of street urchins provided an audience, whooping and cheering. The air was rent with screams from a distraught young girl wearing a green dress. An unconscious man was being tended to by a woman in black clothes, while three men repeatedly lunged forward wielding clubs. Oliver Moon was fighting for his life. He evaded one man and landed a tremendous blow on the side of his head, knocking him senseless. A punch to the stomach by Oliver winded Banks, and he doubled up. Unfortunately, Oliver was tiring, and as he spun around to face Hastings, he tripped and sprawled on the ground. Hastings saw his chance. He kicked Oliver several times in the ribs and then raised his club.

Afterwards, Jake could not explain why he did it. He had never done anything like it before. He had been edging forwards, drawn in horror towards the spectacle before him and then, as Hastings paused, relishing the moment when he would finish off Oliver Moon with a blow from his club, Jake rushed towards Hastings and hit him on the head. Hard. With the back of his iron hook! For a second, Hastings stood motionless, then the club slipped from his hand and he slumped in a heap. Banks, whom Oliver had punched in the stomach, was still bent over, gasping for breath, but realising he no longer had the advantage, he turned and scuttled away to a chorus of jeers from the street urchins who had been enjoying the brawl.

Charlotte stopped screaming; there was a deathly silence, and Jake took in the scene. Hastings, his companion and Carrington lay still on the ground, and Oliver, holding his side, was struggling to his feet.

'Is he alive?' asked Charlotte.

'Yes, just,' replied Carrington's sister, Cissie. 'We must

get him inside.'

'I'll do it,' said Oliver, Ow!'

'Are you alright, Mr Moon?' asked Jake.

'I think I have a few cracked ribs.' Between them, Oliver, Jake, Cissie and Charlotte managed to bear Carrington inside the house.

'I don't know what just happened,' said Cissie.

'It's all my fault,' said Charlotte. 'My father must have sent those men to find me. They work for him.'

'I'm as much to blame,' said Oliver. 'If I had come as soon as I heard they were looking for you instead of staying for a few more drinks, then this may never have happened.'

'We don't have time for working out whose fault it is,' asserted Jake. 'Banks got away, so I'm sure more of Fotheringay's men will return. Maybe he will even send soldiers. We need to get away from here.'

'It's not your fight, Milko. Can't you just slip away?' asked Oliver.

'I'm involved now,' said Jake sadly. 'Only one person has a hand like mine, and that's me. I live in a room owned by the Steam Works. They can easily find me.'

'Then we will stick together, young man. The Rookery is losing its appeal for me anyway,' declared Oliver.

'Can I join you?' asked Charlotte. Jake and Oliver both raised their eyebrows in surprise. 'I hereby renounce my family. I want nothing more to do with a family that can countenance such violence against innocent people.'

'Well, I, Ermm!' responded Jake. He was astonished at the suggestion that he and Oliver join forces but even more amazed that a girl from a wealthy family should also want to share his company.

'It will be an honour to have you along,' said Oliver, settling the matter.

'You should go, and quickly' said Cissie, 'Don't tell me where. They will be back. If I don't know, I can't tell them.' Charlotte grasped Cisse's hand:

'Look after Carry; I'll be in touch.'

'I can't go without my notebooks, new hand, and tools,' stuttered Jake.

'Then lead on, my boy.' The odd little group emerged to see that Hastings and his companions were still out cold, although minus their boots. No doubt someone had relieved them of their purses too.

'Are they alive?' asked Charlotte.

Oliver considered for a moment:

'They may be, or they may not be. I suggest we don't hang around to find out. Which way, Milko?'

'Erm, if we are to be companions, I'd much rather you called me by my name - Jake. We have to go down that alleyway opposite.'

'Right you are, Jakey-boy, so this is the plan; we'll walk as though we are going past it, then I'll create a diversion, and we'll double back. Hopefully, those kids won't notice where we have gone.'

Jake and Charlotte followed Oliver as instructed. They stopped, and Oliver plunged a hand into the pocket of his leather coat and drew out a handful of change, mostly farthings, halfpennies and threepenny bits. 'Here you are, have a drink on me!' He threw the money as far as he could. The reaction was immediate; a throng of street urchins descended on the coins, tussling and scuffling, oblivious to Oliver, Jake and Charlotte, who quickly ran down the alleyway.

'I imagine the thugs offered one of those urchins a penny to show them where you went, Charlotte,' said Oliver.

'I can't tell you how truly sorry I am to have caused all this trouble,' panted Charlotte.

'Think nothing of it. Life has to be an adventure, or it's not worth living!' replied Oliver cheerfully. If she had heard this romantic statement the previous day, Charlotte would have wholeheartedly agreed with the sentiment. Right now, in a cold and dirty alleyway, with darkness descending, she felt far from being adventurous. As he walked, Jake was preoccupied with planning what tools and notebooks he would retrieve from his room. However, he did notice as they passed a public house, that Oliver appeared to pause for a moment but then lengthened his stride and continued with a determined look on his face.

Finally, they arrived at Jake's home, and after scanning the street for observers, they slipped inside.

'Goodness!' gasped Charlotte, seeing the drawings, notes and formulae that adorned the walls. Oliver chuckled as he studied them.

'I hope you're not planning to bring a whole wall with you,' he laughed.

'No, no! I have copies in my notebooks,' replied Jake, failing to see any humour in the situation. Five minutes later, he announced: 'That's it. I've got all the important things - my books, my specialist tools which fortunately are all quite small, and of course, the hand I have been working on.'

'I am concerned about you, Charlotte,' said Oliver. 'You don't exactly blend in. Your dress is extremely pretty, but it looks out of place. It belongs in high society, not on the streets of a London slum, but I know someone who can probably help!

'Well, goodbye then,' said Jake to his neighbour, Molly Scratchit. 'And thank you for all you have done for me over the years.'

'Look after yourself, young Jake. You're a good boy. I know your parents would have been proud of you.'

'I won't tell you where I'm going because I honestly don't know. In any case, Fotheringay's men are bound to come round asking questions.' Jake had ensured that Charlotte and Oliver had walked ahead so that Molly could honestly swear that she had not seen a man in a leather coat and a young lady in a green dress.

'Fotheringay! Curse his name. He'll get no help from me!'

Twenty minutes later, Jake was feeling extremely uncomfortable. He was sitting alone in the front parlour of Madame Boo-Boo's. Oliver had introduced Charlotte to a young woman called Sadie and explained that Charlotte needed a new outfit, and then he had gone to say farewell to another lady in an upstairs room, called Trixie. He seemed to be taking rather a long time!

Meanwhile, Charlotte stood in her undergarments as Sadie held up a selection of dresses.

'They 'aven't got the quality of your dress, Miss Charlotte. I would save wearin' that for special occasions. I can think of one gentleman caller who might call a lot more often if I were wearin' it, if you know what I mean,' said Sadie. Charlotte gave a thin smile; she preferred not to think about the adventures her dress would get up to in the future.

'I don't suppose you have something a little less…bold?' she faltered.

'Well, there is only this one,' replied Sadie. 'I only wear it if I have to go on an errand, if you want to call it that, and I don't want to attract any attention. You can button it all the way up.' Charlotte nodded and took the dress. Sadie continued as Charlotte put it on. 'What you going to do about your hair? It's too clean and shiny. Ee, lass, I'd kill to have curls like that!' Charlotte spotted a pair of scissors on the dressing table and quickly moved across the room to pick them up. Then, to Sadie's astonishment, she grasped a long ringlet and chopped it off. 'I only meant, are you going to have one of my scarves or a bonnet.'

'A new start.' said Charlotte, firmly.

'Well, it's a bit drastic. Ecky thump, you're makin' a reet mess o' that. Let me 'elp. You know, if you are looking to stay out of sight, I'm sure Madame Boo-Boo could fit you in here. You wouldn't have to leave your room very often. To be honest, most of us spend a lot of our time in our rooms, but that's the nature of the business.'

'Thank you for your suggestion, but, erm, I don't think I have the attributes to do your job.'

'Oh, it's easy. You know what men are like!'

'That's just it. I don't.'

At last, Sadie finished the transformation. Charlotte went downstairs to the front parlour, followed by Sadie, to find that Jake was the only one there. He was studying one of his notebooks and gave them the quickest of glances, then looked away in embarrassment. He didn't appear to recognise Charlotte. Oliver came downstairs.

'It's painful saying goodbyes when you've got broken ribs,' he said cheerfully. 'I don't think I've got the energy to say goodbye to you too, Sadie.' Oliver was more observant than Jake, particularly regarding women, and chuckled. 'My, you've done a good job, Sadie. I think she'll blend in now.' Jake followed Oliver's gaze, and his jaw dropped. Now he recognised Charlotte. Oliver clapped his hands. 'So, my fine companions, let us leave The Rookery and seek new adventure!'

'Ahh!' he sighed a short time later as they peered from a dark passageway. Ahead of them were the wrought iron gates through which they would have to pass, but a line of soldiers barred the way. In the distance, a church bell sounded the hour. 'I do believe they are the only gates out of The Rookery!'

'That's true,' replied Jake, 'But there is another way. It means going to the last place they would think to look for us.'

CHAPTER THREE

'Damnation!' yelled Fotheringay as he flung a heavy inkwell onto the floor. It smashed, scattering shards of glass and creating an ever-increasing pool of black ink. His secretary knocked timidly on the door. 'Yes!' Fotheringay shouted irritably.

'Field Marshal Bellings to see you, Sir.'

'Coming right out, we are going on a tour of the factory. Clean up that mess in there before I get back.' Fotheringay walked briskly to the reception room.

A stout elderly man in a red uniform with a sash and rows of medals was waiting for him. Being of the highest rank possible in the British Army, he clearly wanted nobody to be uncertain of his status.

'Fotheringay!' he bellowed.

'Field Marshal Bellings. I have been looking forward to showing you our factory.'

'You've been having a hard day, I hear.'

'Yes, it's my daughter, we can't locate her.'

'Absent without leave, I believe. Or is it desertion we are talking about?'

'I don't know. The men I sent to retrieve my daughter discovered her in The Rookery, but ruffians brutally attacked them.'

'We have a cordon of soldiers around the entrance. She won't get through there,' replied Bellings confidently, 'We will be sending in armed patrols to conduct house-to-house searches very soon. We would have carried them out before now, but the damnedest thing is that every single horse in the army is sick. Cavalry and transport animals. Anyway, when we find this rogue daughter of yours, I would suggest a spell in the glasshouse.'

'Glasshouse? What's that?'

'Oh, it's what we call a military prison. You need to be firm. Set an example.'

'Don't you worry about that, although we will find a more discreet place for her than a glasshouse! I know of a sanatorium where we can keep our eye on her. Anyway, you didn't come here to talk about my daughter. You came to see how the British Army and Fotheringay's Steam Works can forge a new alliance.' A bell rang out, interrupting their conversation.

'Confound it! What's that racket?' asked Bellings.

'It signals a shift change. It means the corridors will be full of workers. I suggest we wait a little while before I show you around. You wouldn't want to be brushing shoulders with them. A brandy, perhaps?'

Jake hid his hook beneath the sack containing his

notebooks and tools. In her new clothes, Charlotte looked fairly nondescript, but Oliver Moon, in his long, leather coat, strode in through the door to Fotheringay's Steam Works with a confident swagger. He didn't even attempt to hide his goggles, although he had removed his top hat, yet he was completely ignored by the long queue of employees filing through the factory door. It was almost as though he were invisible!

Once they were inside Jake tugged Oliver's arm.

'This way,' he whispered. Oliver and Charlotte followed him down a corridor to the left of the factory entrance, while the other workers carried on ahead to the steam plants. 'I know every inch of this factory because I've cleaned most of it. This route will take us around the building to the front entrance door without going past the reception area and Fotheringay's office. Sorry Charlotte, I mean your father's office.'

'I don't want to refer to him as father any longer. I have seen another side to him now. I can't reconcile the poverty in The Rookery with the wealth that he lavishes on himself and his family. I want nothing more to do with him!'

'That's my girl!' laughed Oliver, 'A bit of spirit about you. Brings colour to your cheeks and fire to your belly!'

'I'm not sure I want my stomach to catch fire, thank you very much.' They stopped. From around a corner, ahead of them, came the sound of voices.

'Father's coming!' gasped Charlotte.

'I thought you weren't going to call him father?' retorted Oliver.

'Quick, in here,' whispered Jake, 'It's the Design Room. There's a storeroom at the end where they keep the ink and the paper. We can hide in there until they have gone.'

Unfortunately, the Design Room was also the destination of Fotheringay and Field Marshal Bellings.

'I'll show you the designs first. I asked for them to be left out on display. Normally, as you can imagine, they are kept secret,' said Fotheringay. 'I have two teams working on different aspects of the plans. Very few people know that when we combine this technology, we will produce the deadliest weapon the world has ever known. We call it Tiberius.'

'And it's all powered by steam?'

'Precisely. We are ready to build a prototype.'

'Good man. I can't say I understand all these scratches and squiggles, but I like the sound of it.'

'Now, I'll show you the rest of the factory to demonstrate that we have the capacity to build it.'

From the storeroom, Jake, Oliver and Charlotte heard the sound of the Design Room door shutting.

'Wait here,' said Jake. 'I must look at this,' and he pulled out a notebook and a pencil, peeked around the storeroom door and went out to inspect the designs laid out on the desks. He was excited; he had seen many of them before, but there were new ones here too, and as he copied them, various elements that had puzzled him previously now became clear. Suddenly, just as he was closing the notebook, the door burst open.

'Hooky! What are you doing here?'

'Erm..I was asked to tidy this room up, Mr Grimes, on account of Mr Fotheringay showing someone around. Some army chap.'

'Well, hurry up about it. You should be in the main plant room. It's in a right old mess!'

'Nearly finished, Sir,' called Jake after the supervisor,

who was stomping angrily down the corridor. Jake waited until the coast was clear and retrieved Charlotte and Oliver. Charlotte was nearly petrified with fear at being in such close proximity to her father, whereas Oliver, who seemed oblivious to the danger, sat on the floor rubbing his bruised and broken ribs.

The three arrived at the front entrance without further incident, where they paused to assess the situation. Three soldiers stood guard outside the building.

'I reckon I can take two of them, even with these broken ribs, and you can bash the other one on the head with your hook, Jakey-boy,' said Oliver confidently.

'No!' cried Charlotte, 'That will only make things worse.' At that moment, new-found confidence flowed into her. It was almost as though she had immersed herself in a mountain stream and emerged with a clear mind. 'Wait here!' She strode forward to speak to the soldiers guarding the door. One thing that Charlotte was renowned for was her excellence at parlour games. She had a skill for performing in small dramatic sketches using a range of different accents. She was fluent in French, Italian and German, but now she attempted to imitate Sadie from Madame Boo-Boo's.

'Ere, you've got to come quick! Mr Fotheringay sent me. There's a fearful fight in t' steam room, an' he needs all the help he can get. They got that girl wi' 'em.'

'But what about the door?' asked one of the soldiers.

'He said to bolt it from the inside.' Quickly, the soldiers did as she instructed.

'Which way?' They rushed off in the direction Charlotte pointed. Once they were out of sight, she calmly unbolted the door and held it open for Jake and Oliver, and they all ventured out into the cold, crisp evening.

'The streets are very quiet,' observed Oliver. 'Why, there are no hansom cabs, no hackney carriages, in fact, not a horse to be seen. So it's fitting that it looks like it's Shank's Pony for us.'

'What does that mean?' asked Charlotte.

'Oh, it's a saying we use in Scotland. It means we have to walk.'

'Are you Scottish?' asked Jake.

'Not exactly, although I do have some connections there, but that's another story!'

'And where is Shank's Pony taking us?' enquired Charlotte.

'I've two places in mind. First of all, there's a shop nearby. The owners live on the premises and work all hours. They will still be open.' Twenty minutes later, they were standing in front of the small shop.

'Watson and Sons. Purveyor of finest luggage' read out Jake. Whilst Charlotte took the ability to read for granted, she was aware that very few of the inhabitants of The Rookery were literate. Then again, she was beginning to realise that Jake was unlike the other residents. Oliver rapped on the door, and a whiskery old man wearing a leather apron opened it.

'Well, I do declare, it's Mr Moon. Are you off on your travels again, Sir? Where are you going this time? Come in, come in.' He ushered them into a small dark room smelling of leather and polish. Jake was immediately drawn to a workbench where a range of leather-working tools were laid out neatly in a row.

'I need a large trunk,' said Oliver, 'I remember I purchased one from you when I was posted to India. Have you anything we can take away now? No time for you to make something bespoke.'

'As it happens, Mr Moon, I do have a spare trunk. I made it for a gentleman who had the misfortune to die before he could collect it. I don't know which of us was the more upset about the situation. He hadn't paid me.'

'Splendid! I shall take it off your hands,' replied Oliver cheerfully. Add it to my account and I'll settle up tomorrow when the banks are open.'

Soon the party was continuing their journey, walking towards The Strand. Jake had put his sack inside the trunk, which he and Oliver now carried between them.

'We are here!' Oliver announced, stopping outside a hotel. 'I've been here before. It's rather basic, but it will suffice.' Oliver had evidently forgotten the fact that he had spent the night before sleeping on the pavement. 'I'm afraid Charlotte, you must share the burden of carrying the trunk. It wouldn't be fitting for me to do it, and we don't want to attract attention.' As he marched towards the desk, Jake whispered to Charlotte:

'As if a man wearing a full-length leather coat, a silk scarf and goggles is not likely to attract attention!'

'Good evening. Mr Moon, I do believe. Do you require a room?'

'I need a suite if you have one. Three beds.' He gestured towards Jake and Charlotte. 'I prefer my servants to be close at hand. Are we too late for any food? I'm famished!'

Jake gasped when he saw the suite. He had lived all his life in a single room, yet here was a large bedroom, two smaller bedrooms and a bathroom linked to a drawing room with tall windows overlooking the street. A servant brought up a tray bearing bread, a selection of cold meats, a pot of tea for Jake and Charlotte, and a bottle of brandy for Oliver. There was little conversation. At first, they were too hungry, and then exhaustion set in. Oliver graciously offered Charlotte the largest bedroom. As she and Jake were retiring to their beds Oliver called out to them:

'I have a few things to sort out tomorrow. I suggest you stay up here until things settle down. I can arrange for some food to be sent up for you. Goodnight, I'll just have another drop of this brandy.'

Jake lay on his bed. Unusually for him, his thoughts were swirling around, and he was finding it difficult to focus on one thing for long. Normally he could function very well, letting his brain wrestle with an engineering problem whilst he methodically swept the factory. Thoughts fluttered around his mind like trapped moths. On the one hand he was now homeless, unemployed and on the run. If he was caught he would surely be hanged! On the other hand, he had seen exciting new diagrams in the Design Room. 'On the other hand,' he thought. 'That's a good expression because I've still got my other hand to finish!' It was all very confusing!

Charlotte could not get to sleep straight away either, even though she was extremely tired. When she had woken up earlier that morning in the imposing mansion overlooking Hyde Park, she couldn't have predicted that she would end the day sharing a hotel suite with two men she had never seen before. She had experienced such a range of emotions. After talking to her parents, she had been angry, and then in The Rookery, she had been frightened, but for a brief moment, when Charlotte tricked the soldiers into leaving their post, she had felt brave.

'Am I being foolhardy and naive?' she thought, 'Or are these the first steps in fulfilling my destiny?'

CHAPTER FOUR

'I hope you have some good news to report, Hetherington,' barked Fotheringay.

'Erm, I'm afraid not, but I thought you ought to know something straight away,' stammered the Chief Designer.

'Know what? Out with it! Have you found her?'

'Erm... erm, no, we haven't, but one of Hastings' team asked me to visit a certain individual's house, a cleaner here at the factory.'

'A cleaner!' Fotheringay exploded, 'Don't tell me the stupid girl has run off with a cleaner! I'm in two minds whether to wash my hands of the matter and let her go hang!'

'No, no, Sir. I mean, I don't know if she has. All I know is that this boy, Jake Moss, is involved. They call him

Hooky, and it was he that hit Hastings on the head. We identified the assailant because he had a hook instead of his left hand. I was called to look at his room because of what he had drawn on the walls. The soldiers wondered if there might be any clues about where they had gone.'

'And were there?'

'No, Sir.'

'Then why are you wasting my time?'

'Sir, Sir, what was drawn on the walls is the issue, Sir. They were very accurate drawings of Tiberius.'

'Tiberius!' yelled Fotheringay. But that's a secret! How is that possible?'

'It's possible, Sir, because he used to clean Design Room, and I'm afraid it gets worse. Banks saw him there after Field Marshal Bellings had visited, when the final drawings were spread out on the tables .'

'Damnation! Who let this spy into our midst? Heads will roll. We need to find him and put an end to him. Get me Hastings. Oh, no, he's incapacitated. Did he live?'

'Yes, Sir. He's in the hospital, recovering.'

'Well, he can just get up from his bed and do his job properly. Find this Hooky fellow, and find him now! We can't risk details about Tiberius falling into our rivals' hands.'

'Or the enemy, Sir.'

'Obviously!'

'And your daughter, Sir. Should he look for her too?'

'Yes, of course. She might lead us to him.'

Charlotte emerged from the bathroom. It was the first time in her life that she had put on the same dirty clothes that she had worn the day before. She realised this would be the first of many changes in her life. Jake was already up and busy working on his mechanical hand.

'Good morning, Jake,' she said. The tremor in her voice betrayed her nervousness. It was a completely new situation for her. Charlotte was used to talking to family members in the mornings and knew what tone to take with servants, but this? The previous day had been so full of action and tension that Jake and Charlotte hadn't had time to consider how to converse and interact with each other. Now Jake mumbled a greeting but did not make eye contact. At first, Charlotte thought he was being rude, but then she noticed that his ears were starting to redden and she realised that he, too, was nervous. 'Is Mr Moon still asleep?'

'No,' replied Jake. 'I heard him go out first thing this morning. Quite surprising, really.' He gestured towards the empty brandy bottle lying on its side.

There was a knock on the door; Jake opened it to reveal a servant holding a breakfast tray.

'Compliments of Mr Moon,' said the servant. 'I'm sorry, but we haven't had our usual delivery this morning, so we don't have any kippers, but there is plenty of eggs, bacon and toast. Unfortunately, today's newspapers aren't here either. I can't think what's going wrong this morning! Enjoy your breakfast. Oh, and don't worry about a gratuity; Mr Moon has already given me a tip.'

'What is your name?'

'It's Tom, Miss.'

'Thank you, Tom,' said Charlotte. 'We appreciate your efforts.' Jake could only nod effusively. The breakfast in store for him would be a feast. His usual fare was a hunk of stale bread and a glass of milk. Tom left the room thinking Charlotte was the prettiest and most well-spoken maid he had ever met.

Jake moved his tools and mechanical hand to one side so they had enough room to eat. Breakfast was mainly conducted in silence. After the first few mouthfuls, Jake, following Charlotte's example, concentrated on trying not to eat too fast.

'More tea?' said Charlotte a little while later, reaching for Jake's cup. Unfortunately, in doing so, she nudged one of the cogs standing on its end at the edge of the table, and it rolled off and out of sight.

'Oh no!' gasped Jake. It was a calamity! He needed every part. That cog was vital!

'I'm so sorry,' cried Charlotte, dropping to the floor to search for it. Jake crawled underneath the table as well to look for his precious cog. Then, after a few minutes, Charlotte spied it resting against the inside of the table leg. She held it out for Jake, who took it gratefully and smiled. Then she giggled, picturing the absurdity of the situation - sitting under a table in a strange hotel room with a young man. Jake joined in, and they remained under the table for five minutes, laughing uncontrollably. From that moment onwards, they were friends.

Later that morning, Jake was sitting at the table making the last few adjustments to his prosthetic hand, while Charlotte gazed out of the tall sash window that overlooked the street.

'Jake, just look at this!' Jake joined her at the window, and they watched a handcart being pulled very slowly by a pair of straining men. It was loaded up with two dead horses. Behind it came a similar cart, only this time it bore a donkey and a mule.

'There must be an abattoir somewhere near,' said Jake.

'I don't think I've seen a single horse since I took a

hansom cab to the factory yesterday, and even that one was sick!'

'It's all very, very strange, Charlotte. It's like our whole world has turned upside down!' Charlotte returned to her study of the street.

'I've finished,' said Jake, holding up his metal hand, 'Would you mind helping me get my hook off?' Then followed another new experience in Charlotte's life, struggling to twist the hook off the end of Jake's wrist. Until now, she had avoided staring at it, thinking it would be rude, but now she had no choice.

'I'm sorry it's so hard to get off,' apologised Jake, 'It's been on a long time.'

'Goodness! Oh, at last! It's off! I hope I didn't hurt you.'

'It's a little sore, but I've designed this one to be much easier to remove,' said Jake, clipping the new hand into place. 'I've ideas for a whole range of them with different purposes.' Charlotte stared at the hand as Jake took a key, inserted it into the back and wound it up. It seemed the hand had a clockwork mechanism. There was a row of buttons running across it and Charlotte could see that the fingers were all individually jointed. The whole thing was a gleaming mix of brass and steel.

'Why! It's quite beautiful,' said Charlotte. 'It looks so intricate, so well engineered!'

'Thank you,' said Jake. 'Would you like to see it in action?' He proceeded to press combinations of buttons, making each finger extend or the whole hand clench. 'If I activate this button,' he explained, 'The movement will stop when it makes contact with something and not carry on and crush it. I thought it would be useful for when I picked up my sweeping brush, but I suppose those days are over.'

Just then, there was a knock on the door. Jake opened it, and Tom burst into the room. It took him a few seconds to get his breath back.

'Sorry, I ran up the stairs as fast as I could. I came to tell you that some soldiers have been to the hotel asking if I had seen a young man with a hook instead of a hand, a lady, possibly wearing a green dress, and a man in a leather coat. The manager isn't here now, he's at the bank, so they are coming back later. I just thought you ought to know. Mr Moon has always been very good to me, but I couldn't help noticing you had a hook, Sir.' Jake held up his metal hand and smiled:

'Call me Jake, Tom.'

'Very nice, Jake, Not a hook, and your dress definitely isn't green, Miss. Anyway, I wanted to warn you but don't worry. If they come back I shan't tell them anything. Wait on! I've had an idea. Back in a minute,' and he rushed out of the room.

Meanwhile, Jake and Charlotte stared out the window, watching as an army patrol visited every house in the street. A moment later, Tom was back, even more breathless than before. He held out a pair of large leather gloves.

'I thought these might be useful,' he panted, 'They used to belong to one of the chefs, only he moved on and left them behind. They don't fit anyone else because his hands are so big, but they might be useful for you, Jake.'

'I think I had better put my tools and notebooks back in the trunk in case we have to make a quick exit,' said Jake once Tom had left.

A nervous hour passed. Jake tried to study one of his notebooks but couldn't concentrate. Charlotte paced up and down. She gasped when they heard the doorknob rattle, but it was only Oliver, who strode into the room carrying a bundle of clothing.

'I know, I know,' he said, raising a hand. 'Tom told me. It won't change our plans. A generous tip to the manager will keep the hounds from our door - first, a drop of brandy. Hair of the dog, you know. Does wonders! I've brought you overcoats. Take a look.' Whilst Charlotte and Jake unwrapped the bundle of clothing, Oliver poured himself a drink and stretched out on the chaise. He certainly wasn't in any hurry.

'Strange doings out there, my friends,' said Oliver, 'You may have noticed an absence of horses on the street. Well, I've seen plenty, a big pile of 'em. They are making big bonfires of dead horses in Hyde Park. They say it's some kind of influenza. The horses started sneezing and having difficulty breathing, and then they keeled over and died. As a result, a lot of the shops are running out of stock because they aren't getting supplies delivered to them. I've seen people fighting in the queues to buy bread. There are soldiers on the streets to keep order, as well as soldiers looking for us. I reckon things could turn very ugly. I've brought you a present, Charlotte - something to keep hidden.' Oliver took a small, silver pistol engraved with ornamental patterns from his pocket. 'Just in case we get into another sticky situation. I shouldn't think it would stop a rabbit at five yards, but it might come in handy if we get into a tight corner.'

Oliver looked Jake and Charlotte up and down. They were both wearing their new overcoats. 'Very elegant indeed, I guessed the sizes correctly. And your hand, Jake, it's very…handsome!' Oliver smiled at his little joke and poured himself another drink. Then, over the top of his leather coat, he put on a full-length, checked gaberdine coat extravagantly trimmed with fur. 'I just couldn't resist it.

What do you think?'

'It's beautiful. I don't think we resemble at all the people the soldiers are searching for,' said Charlotte

'True. But I want to be clear. I bought this coat because I liked it before I knew the soldiers were looking for a man in a leather coat. I wouldn't want you to think my fashion choices were due to fear of being identified!'

'Neither of us would think that, Mr Moon,' said Jake. Charlotte nodded in agreement.

'You can call me Oliver, Jakey-boy,' said Oliver. 'No, I've bought coats because we are going quite a long way North. It will be cold.'

'How will we get there?' asked Charlotte, 'If there are no horses.'

'Oh! Didn't I tell you? I own an airship.'

CHAPTER FIVE

The Cavalry Club on Piccadilly, Mayfair.

'So, you are saying there is no progress?' said Field Marshal Bellings. He couldn't disguise the anger bubbling up inside him. He wasn't having a good day. 'You create the most powerful weapon the world has ever seen, and then you let some itinerant worker waltz off with the plans for it?'

'Can your men not redouble their efforts to find him?' asked Fotheringay. He was equally frustrated, furious that he found himself in this position. He wasn't a man to apologise. 'We never dreamt that a cleaner would have the intelligence to make sense of the plans.'

'Never dreamt? Never mind dreaming; this is turning into a nightmare! I've deployed all the men I can spare. The country is on a knife edge. The masses are complaining, and I have problems within my ranks. I was a cavalryman. That's why I am a member of The Cavalry Club. We are the elite! What are my men supposed to do if they do not have horses to ride?'

'If possible, we need to capture this spy alive,' said Fotheringay. 'We need to determine whether he passed the plans on to a third party - another factory or a foreign power. Then, when we know the facts, he must disappear quietly and permanently. We do not want the matter to go through the courts. You, personally, are going to gain financially from the production of Tiberius. You do not want that fact to become public. Now, tell me about this other fellow. The man in the leather coat who had the audacity to stroll through my factory.'

'Ah! That's Oliver Moon. I took great pleasure in drumming him out of the army. He's a thoroughly bad apple with no regard for discipline and authority. Make no mistake, we shall find him. We shall find them all.'

Edward

I know it might sound prestigious, being a reporter for The Times, but I'm not fooling myself. Most of what I write is entirely inconsequential and I have no way of knowing whether anyone reads my articles. Mostly, they are dry reports on parliamentary affairs or obituaries of people who have led mediocre lives. I've always had difficulty positioning myself within the literary world. I worked hard at University, but I knew then that I could never aspire to high art. I will never be a Keats or a Byron. I have neither the talent nor the private income to allow me to pursue that goal. Sitting before a blank piece of paper, I would sooner write a limerick than compose a sonnet.

So, here I am at the Times, a post I gained purely through the influence of my father-in-law, Sir Robert Ford. I wonder if I would be treated with more respect if I were a rich man in my own right. My father was a humble minister, the kind of man who would give away every penny he had to the poor, so when he died unexpectedly, there was little to pass on to me. I didn't even inherit his house, as the vicarage belonged to the church. I met Arabella at a garden party - her parents owned a weekend retreat in the village. She is extremely wealthy, having been left a large inheritance, but I didn't know that when I fell in love with her.

When my father died, we were already married and living in our London house, purchased by my wife's father as a wedding present. I was still full of youthful dreams of writing pieces that would unmask villains and put the world to rights. Not that Sir Robert approved of my profession. He still thinks that any day now I will give it up and join him in the banking world. I wouldn't put it past him to have spoken with my editor to ensure I do not rise through the ranks. So, having the Fords in my life is driving a wedge between Arabella and me. She sides increasingly with their point of view, and I find myself becoming more and more isolated. If I could, I would express my feelings, but my wife and her family have made it very clear that a Victorian gentleman does not give way to weak and feeble emotions and must bear up and do his duty.

Edward Ramsey looked down from the Strangers Gallery in the House of Commons at the two squabbling sets of politicians. As a junior reporter for the Times, he was finding this aspect of his job extremely tiresome. Nothing ever seemed to be decided: "My Honourable friend" this and "My Honourable friend" that, blah blah blah! It had been a very unusual day so far, with no horses on the street, so it had taken him a long time to walk from his home in so-called "Toff Town." He didn't like that description; he didn't see himself as a toff.

Edward's pencil was poised above his notebook, but observing the wealthy, self-serving politicians bickering below gave him no inspiration to write anything. Walking through the streets, Edward had felt something ugly in the air, and the politicians either were not in touch with ordinary people or, worse, - they knew what was happening and chose to ignore it! He had enough information to write his piece later. If he wanted to get to the bottom of things, where better to go than somewhere these despicable men would fear to tread? He would go to The Rookery.

'There's a lot of people walking this evening,' said Tom as he pulled a handcart loaded with possessions belonging to Oliver, Jake and Charlotte. 'You wouldn't normally see so many toffs on the street. Some of 'em have got a right cob on by the look of their sour faces. What's that song you are whistling, Mr Moon?'

'It's a marching song from my army days,' replied Oliver, tapping his new walking cane on the pavement to emphasise the beat.

'Very, jaunty, if you don't mind me saying so. And all of you look splendid!'

'I've never even owned a pair of gloves before,' confessed Jake as he pressed the buttons on his metal hand and enjoyed the effect of moving his fingers. 'And now, wearing my new overcoat, I simply wouldn't recognise myself!'

Charlotte focused on her steps and her breath, keeping time to the tapping of Oliver's cane and clearing her mind to banish all the feelings of panic and self-doubt that bubbled below the surface.

'After all,' she thought, 'I'm going to travel in an

airship. It's what I've always wanted.'

'Here we are - The River Thames,' announced Tom. 'I'll find someone to row you and help load the luggage onto the boat. Very popular they are for getting around since the horse flu came.'

Tom went home humming the same tune Oliver had been whistling, with the comforting bulge of money hidden in his sock. Meanwhile, on the boat journey to East London, Oliver, Jake, and Charlotte had agreed not to let slip any clues about their final destination. They didn't know if the ferryman was to be trusted.

'Jake, we'll take the trunk between us if you can carry the basket of provisions, Charlotte,' said Oliver as they alighted from the boat.

'Welcome to Blackwall,' read Jake, from a sign at the top of the steps leading from the river.

'Welcome to Blackwall, indeed,' replied a sinister voice from the shadows. 'We are The Wild Boys, and you are on our patch.' Three men in their twenties stepped out from the darkness. 'What's in the trunk?'

'Just some notebooks, some clothes and a few tools,' replied Jake. 'I'll show you.' Jake quickly undid the lock to the trunk, opened it and stepped back.

'Pah! That ain't worf nuffin'. In that case, we are goin' to have to relieve you of your purses.'

'Ah! That simply won't do!' said Oliver politely. 'Firstly, I must point out that my colleague here has a fearsome punch. You should see his left jab. Show them, Jake,' and he gestured with his cane towards the wooden sign welcoming them to Blackwall. Jake responded immediately, and the Wild Boys were astonished to see Jake hit the sign so hard that his gloved metal fist burst through it. 'Then, of course, there is this!' said Oliver, withdrawing a slender sword from his cane. Taking her cue, Charlotte took out the pistol from her basket and pointed it directly at the gang leader.

'And you will also have to deal with this,' she said firmly. Inside she was shaking, but it didn't show. By now, Jake was brandishing his fist and Oliver was smiling, quite happy at the prospect of a fight. The combined show of force proved effective; the gang members mumbled something inaudible to each other and melted back into the shadows. Oliver put a finger to his lips to signal silence. He knew better than to jeer or mock and so provoke them into returning with reinforcements.

'Onward, my good friends,' he announced, and they continued their journey. Oliver began to whistle once more. Jake and Charlotte looked at each other; that had been a close shave and they were visibly shaking, but after a few moments, they both relaxed and started to smile.

Edward was curious. Why were there were so many red-coated soldiers searching The Rookery? Usually, this neighbourhood was left to look after its own affairs. His first enquiry did not get off to a good start.

'Good day, my name is Edward Ramsey, from the Times, and I wonder if you would be so good to enlighten me as to...'

'Reporter, eh! Keep yer nose out!' interrupted the soldier.

Edward found a fairly clean section of a low wall and sat on it to watch the proceedings. He pulled a penny bun from a paper bag. As he was eating he found that he had an audience. A small boy stood in front of him and watched him intently.

'Would you like one?' asked Edward and he held out a bun. The boy grabbed it eagerly and stuffed it in his mouth. 'Who or what are they looking for?' asked Edward, nodding towards the soldiers.

'They're looking for Hooky,'

'Who or what is Hooky?'

'He's a chap what cleans at the Steam Works. Gimme another bun an' I'll show you 'is house.'

'Take me there first, and then I'll give you a bun.' Ten minutes later, after winding through a maze of back streets and passageways, they arrived at the small house where Jake had a room. Feeling generous, Edward gave the rest of the buns to the boy, who promptly ran off, intending to eat them all before a bigger boy forced him to hand them over. Seeing an open door, Edward approached the house and tentatively crept in. He smelt fresh paint and could hear the sound of two men chatting.

'Hello,' said Edward.

'Wotcher!' Two men had almost finished whitewashing a wall. There was just one of Jake's diagrams still visible.

'Ave you come from the Steam Works to check up on us?' said one of the decorators. 'Nearly finished. Just this bit left.' He slapped a brushful of paint over the drawing and it disappeared from view.

'Do you often paint company houses?' asked Edward, deciding not to reveal his profession yet.

'No, course not. I've been workin' twenty years an' I ain't done one before.'

'So why this one?'

'Not our place to ask questions,' replied the other decorator, 'They said we just had to get rid of them funny drawings.'

'What were they?'

'No idea, mate. A load of cogs and springs and the like. Your guess is as good as mine. Now, if it's alright with you, we'll get on and clear up and clear off because we've finished.'

Edward wandered back into the daylight, puzzled. So the soldiers were looking for a chap called Hooky, and the Steam Factory was spending time and effort obliterating a wall full of doodles. It was all very curious. Very odd indeed!

'Here we are, my friends,' announced Oliver. They had walked through a rather desolate area of London, past crumbling warehouses and piles of rusting ironwork. Jake and Charlotte's good mood had evaporated. It wasn't the kind of landscape to inspire confidence. Ahead of them was a large muddy bank. Piled against it were old planks that were probably salvaged from the buildings they had passed. In the centre of the stack was an opening covered with sewn-together hessian sacks. They had passed several encampments where vagrants lived, and this looked like another of them. 'Billy!' Oliver yelled.

A grubby young boy emerged from behind the sacking and peered towards the approaching group.

'Is that you, Mr Moon? 'Ave you come to bring me my wages?'

'It certainly is, my boy. How have you been?'

'Mustn't grumble. The Wild Boys gen'rally leave me alone 'cos they can't find anyfink to nick. I keeps me wages buried, and they ain't got a clue wot we know, Mr Moon! Gets a bit borin', mind. You've been away longer than I 'spected.'

'Well, I got distracted a little, but there's something in

the air, and I believe it's time to leave London.'

'Can I come? I'm a bit fed up.'

'What about your parents? Won't they miss you? I thought you were sending them money.'

'I was, only they used it ter get drunk and got in ter more trouble. Me Mum's in the nick in 'Olloway fer a few years yet, and me old man's on a convict ship goin' ter somewhere called Stralia. Don't reckon he'll be back fer a while.'

'Glad to have you along, my boy. We need another crew member,' said Oliver. 'Allow me to introduce Jake and Charlotte. Come on lads; we've work to do. Let's move all this wood. We'll put it back as best we can afterwards so no one will notice anything has changed. In any case, we may need to come back. And you, Charlotte, we need your help too.' Charlotte didn't protest, although she had never done any physical work in her whole life.

Once the planks were moved to one side, Jake and Charlotte were amazed to see Billy's sparse living space -an iron bedstead, an old chair and an upturned tea chest which he used as a table. The entire back wall was covered, like his front door, with a patchwork of hessian.

'Oliver, just where on earth are we, and where is your airship?' Charlotte asked as they carried Billy's furniture outside. Oliver smiled and pointed to the hessian curtain.

'This is where the Metropolitan Board of Works intend to build a tunnel under the Thames. They have made a start and know that it is viable. They now have to raise more money to continue. In the meantime, it is an excellent place to hide my airship,' Oliver yanked the hessian aside to reveal the gleaming nose of his craft. 'Behold! A thing of beauty.'

The next hour involved even harder work. Oliver

secured a winch to a hook outside the tunnel entrance, and the airship was slowly pulled out of its hiding place. It remained floating a few feet from the ground, anchored by ropes. The airship was mainly cream-coloured, with touches of deep red, and had a black bolt of lightning painted on either side. Below it was suspended a long cabin.

'I know that is called a gondola,' explained Charlotte to Jake, 'And they call the balloon part above the envelope.'

'Have you been in one before?' asked Jake.

'No, but Carrington took me to see one tethered in Regent's Park. I've always wanted to travel in one. The gondola's ivory and maroon paintwork reminds me of the livery of a railway carriage.'

'If you say so,' said Billy, 'I ain't never seen a train.'

'OMG? What does that stand for?' asked Charlotte, noticing the flowing script painted on the door.

'Oliver Moon's Gondola,' said Oliver with a sheepish grin. 'I'm a man of action rather than words. I ought to have a name for the airship, but I haven't thought of anything yet. Anyway, the sooner we replace all the planks to hide the tunnel, the sooner you will be gliding through the air, I want to slip away whilst it's still dark.'

It was an hour later when they finished. Then, finally, Oliver, Jake, Charlotte and Billy climbed a rope ladder to the gondola. With a flick of his wrists, Oliver released the last remaining rope securing the airship to the ground, and slowly and silently, she rose into the night sky.

CHAPTER SIX

Edward walked across Hyde Park from his perfectly respectable, albeit modest home to reach the imposing mansion where the Fotheringays lived. His parents-in-law lived nearby and probably knew the Fotheringays, but he wanted to make his own connections! He knocked on the door and waited. Eventually, a butler opened it.

'Good morning,' announced Edward. 'My name is Edward Ramsey, and I'm with The Times. I wondered if there was any truth to the rumour that Miss Charlotte Fotheringay is missing.'

'Miss Fotheringay is not receiving callers, Good day, Sir,' came the reply, and the door was shut firmly, leaving Edward deflated on the doorstep. As he began to walk away, he saw a maid leaving the property from a side gate, carrying a basket.

'Allow me,' he said, gesturing towards her basket. The maid was flustered; amazed that such a fine-looking gentleman would offer help to a mere servant.

'Oh, thank you very much, Sir, but I can manage. It's quite light. I'm having to collect some supplies because we haven't had a delivery on account of all the horses being sick. Now if you were to ask me on my way back when I'm weighed down, it would be a different matter! What a day it's been!'

'What a day, indeed. What a week!' replied Edward. Then, while he had her attention, he added quickly, 'I'm very worried about Miss Charlotte Fotheringay.'

'We all are. Her bed hasn't been slept in since Tuesday. I couldn't take another week like this. Poor Mr Carrington getting the sack an' all! I heard he's gone to live in The Rookery, and now Miss Charlotte's missing. I hope you find her soon.' The maid began to walk away and Edward hurried to catch up.

'We are doing our best. Do you have any idea where Miss Charlotte might have gone?'

'No, the last place we know she went was the Steam Works. We know because we had to help her get a cab 'cause Mr Carrington couldn't drive her as he had already gone. Such a nice man an' all. He got on with everyone. He was very fond of Miss Charlotte.' They came to a road junction. A row of shops lay straight ahead.

'I'm afraid I need to walk in this direction to get to my office,' said Edward, gesturing to a side road. 'I hope your basket isn't too heavy on your return.'

'I'll manage. I'll have to. Good luck in finding Miss Charlotte. I hope she isn't in any danger.'

'We'll do our best,' Edward repeated, thinking to

himself that the maid had obviously presumed he was a detective. Maybe he would call in on the Bow Street Runners. They were London's finest detectives, after all.

'It looks much bigger on the inside than it did on the outside. It reminds me of being inside a luxury yacht,' said Charlotte.

'I ain't ever been on a luxury yacht,' said Billy, wistfully.

'Nor me,' said Jake, gazing around him.

'Well, it's just like this,' laughed Charlotte,' The way it curves around, with a wheel at the front. Actually, that's called the helm, only on a yacht, the windows don't slope outwards like these.'

'They give a great view of the streets and the river,' said Jake, 'They are getting smaller, so we must be climbing higher.'

'I'm setting the controls to travel North now,' called Oliver from the helm. The airship swung round slowly and the lights of the Thames river traffic slid behind them. 'I know you are interested in air travel, Charlotte, and you shall have a turn at the controls in due course, but for now my advice to you all is to get some sleep. You will be better able to help tomorrow if you are bright and fresh. Stretch out on the benches. She's designed to transport passengers, so it's good to have more people aboard.'

'Sleeping!' thought Charlotte, 'What a fanciful idea. Impossible! It's all too exciting.'

'Bye bye, East End,' called Billy, lying down and facing the window. 'Shame it's all black out there.'

Shortly afterwards, Oliver smiled as he listened to the rhythmical breathing of his three passengers, all fast asleep.

Charlotte was the first to wake. Sunlight streamed

through the windows, silhouetting Oliver at the prow of the gondola.

'Good morning, Oliver,' she said, stretching and yawning, 'I can't think how you have managed to keep going all night.'

'Good morning. It's hard to describe, but when I stand here, it's as though I have become part of the wind that blows us along. It gives me energy, although I must admit I am ready for a rest.' Jake, woken by the sound of voices, joined Charlotte in staring at the array of instruments and controls. Unlike her, he didn't have a burning desire to fly the machine; he just wanted to know how it worked.

'What are they all for?' he asked.

'This lever controls the angle of the two forward propellers,' explained Oliver, 'And these two change their thrust. The joystick on my left commands the rear propellers to make the nose go up and down, or I can use it to make the airship tack from side to side. There are switches, levers and toggles to control the hydrogen's pressure and the ballast distribution. And, of course, there is the compass. As you can see, we are flying north.'

What powers the propellers?' asked Jake, 'Surely it can't be steam?'

'You are quite right. It's a clockwork mechanism. I experimented with a self-winding system operated by an external windmill, but it didn't work. So, every now and then, I have to wind it up manually.'

'I could do that for yer!' Billy was awake now too.

'By all means, Billy, help yourself.'

'Excuse me, but did you say I could … steer the airship?' asked Charlotte.

'I thought you would never ask,' smiled Oliver, and he

gestured for Charlotte to take the wheel. He showed her how to steer by moving the rudder and adjusting the elevators mounted outside, which controlled the angle of ascent or descent.

'It's a bit like sailing a boat,' explained Oliver.

'My father would never let a woman sail a boat,' said Charlotte, ruefully.

'Only instead of underwater currents, air currents and thermals can make her lift or drop,' continued Oliver.

'Am I doing it right?' asked Charlotte.

'Why, you are doing splendidly. We are speeding along at least forty-five miles an hour.' Oliver took a seat nearby and shouted instructions and words of encouragement. Eventually, as Charlotte gained more confidence, Oliver decided to retire to the rear of the airship for a rest, 'Keep her travelling North, Charlotte. Billy, keep winding the clockwork to make the engines work, and Jake, just make yourself useful!'

Billy

All me life, I've been a nobody. Nuffink special. I'm the youngest. I've got a sister and two bruvvers, and it was them that brought me up. Not me mum and dad; they was in and out of the magistrate's court, and we was always one step away from the dosshouse. I'm sure that if any of us kids 'ad ever got nicked, the dosshouse would be where we would have ended up, but somehow we managed to keep our hooters clean. When me sister moved out 'cause she got spliced, me two bruvvers sort of forgot about me. I didn't care for me sister's 'usband, he used to knock me about a bit, so I 'ad to fend for meself.

Priority number one was always grub. Every day I would do me rounds; the bakery, where I might find some crusts that 'ad got burnt in the oven, the market, where at the end of the day, I might find a bit of veg on the ground that I could chuck into a broth. I weren't too proud to sneak round the back of boozers and pick out leftovers from the slops bin. Better it fattened me up than some pig.

It was a blessing the day I met Oliver Moon and started minding 'is airship. 'E give me wages so I could afford to buy grub instead of scroungin' for it. I didn't go barmy, though. 'E weren't exactly reliable in payin' me wages regular, so I ate a lot of spuds, onions and porridge. And bread, of course, although now I could afford to buy some lard or dripping to spread on it. Once a week, I'd buy some meat; pigs trotters were always good value.

I'd always try and be invisible. I wouldn't splash me coins around. I buried the money Oliver Moon give me, so the street gangs wouldn't pinch it, and usually, I'd eat what I bought straight away, 'specially if it were some fancy tucker like jellied eels or cockles. Once they were in me belly, no one could nick 'em!

Anyway, 'ere I am on an airship. I know there's grub in the basket that Charlotte brought. Normally, as soon as no one were lookin', I'd be right in there, but I ain't gonna, I'll wait 'cause I like these people. I ain't a nuffink any more; I'm one of the crew!

Charlotte stood at the helm, making slight adjustments as she felt the airship move sideways, or pitch up or down. Perhaps stormy conditions would call for more dramatic movements, but this clear, sunny morning called for a slow and steady turn of the wheel and tiny adjustments to the array of levers before her. Charlotte understood now what Oliver had talked about.

'It's like it is me being blown along with the wind at my back. I feel I'm floating!' Charlotte thought back to the key points in her life. When, as a girl, she was taken to Paris and managed to order a meal for herself and her parents in

French. When they visited the Uffizi Gallery in Florence, and her breath was taken away by Botticelli's painting of "The Birth of Venus", or when she heard Lucy Anderson, the first woman pianist to play at the Philharmonic Society concerts, playing Beethoven's "Emperor Concerto". Did any of these experiences match up to the sensations she felt now? They weren't even on the same scale. She couldn't feel any closer to heaven.

Jake was in a heaven of his own. So much engineering! He opened side panels in the airship to trace cables, studied how switches were wired and stared intently at the cogs that quietly clicked round, providing the engines with power. He was puzzled, though, as well as excited by what he saw; he felt something was amiss. The design was good, but it wasn't good enough. He had no experience with flying machines, but the basic physics he had learnt from his trips to the British Museum's Reading Room told him he could improve the system. Jake flexed his new hand, admiring the technology. When he had a moment, he wanted to take another look at the drawings he had made on that last day in the Steam Works Design Room. If anyone had been asked a few days ago, they would have said dismissively, 'He's just a cleaner,' but he didn't feel like that now. He saw himself as a design engineer. If heaven existed, he felt he would be able to improve it with the addition of a few springs, gears and cogs!

Billy felt like a caged bird that had been set free. He turned the handle that wound the clockwork mechanism, but his eyes were glued to the ever-changing view out of the windows. Here was he, a boy who had never been out of the East End of London, now flying over fields and rivers and forests. Green had not been a colour that had figured in his previous life. Even the weeds that struggled to survive between the cracks in the pavement in his part of London were black with grime and soot, but now there was green everywhere - in every shade, from emerald trees to jade pasture. They were flying low enough for him to see farmhands working in the fields. Occasionally, one of them would notice the cigar-shaped shadow on the ground and look up as the airship cruised by silently. Billy imagined them open-mouthed in amazement. With the clockwork motor fully wound, he joined Charlotte at the helm, from where he had a better view of what lay ahead rather than just what was directly below.

'Wot's happenin' there?' he asked, pointing to a field in the distance. Jake came to look.

'Are they having some kind of race?' wondered Charlotte. They could see figures running across the field.

'No, it's more serious than that,' said Jake worriedly, 'I think they are chasing someone. Can you go slower and take us further down?' Nervously, Charlotte adjusted the controls and was gratified when the airship responded to her touch.

'We should ask Mr Moon,' said Billy, racing back to where Oliver was snoring. Moments later, he returned, 'I can't wake him. I think it's because he was up all night, and there's an empty bottle of wine in his hand.' By now, the airship was quite low, and they could see the glint of weapons in the sunlight. Some of the pursuers looked like farm labourers, but red-coated soldiers were amongst them too.

'The thing is, whose side are we on?' asked Jake. 'I don't fancy the chances of the chap in front. There's a river ahead. It depends if he can swim.'

'The army hasn't been particularly kind to us lately,' observed Charlotte.

'Then let's help the fox, not the hounds,' said Jake.

'How?' asked Charlotte.

'One of the mooring ropes is still coiled on the winch next to the doorway. You could lower me down. Billy, can you tie a slipknot on the end of that rope so we can make a loop for him to catch hold of? Charlotte, can you travel at the same speed that he is running?' Showing no trace of fear, Jake twisted the knotted rope around his metal hand and pressed a button to make his fingers lock tightly on it. 'Winch me down!' he shouted to Billy, and he opened the gondola door. The flight had seemed quite calm and serene before, but now he was outside being buffeted by the wind he spun round and round. Billy lowered Jake further down - the airship was now travelling just behind the running man. Jake twisted his head round to look at the pursuers. They weren't gaining any ground, but then again, they weren't falling any further. Jake was about to call out to the man they were chasing when he stumbled on a rock and collapsed.

Billy was watching intently and, seeing this development, let out enough rope to lower Jake to the ground.

'Can ya make the airship stop, Charlotte?' he yelled.

'I'll try, but it won't be instant,' she responded as she slammed the controls into reverse.

'I'll let out more rope,' shouted Billy to Jake, although with the wind noise, he realised Jake probably wouldn't hear him.

Jake nearly stumbled, as it wasn't until he hit the ground that he realised how fast they had been travelling. He didn't have much time. The pack was nearly on its quarry. Jake slipped the loop around the dead weight of the man's body, which started to bounce along the ground as the rope pulled taut. Now Jake was left behind. That hadn't been part of his plan! He ran to catch up. By now, the man he had rescued was dangling a few feet from the ground. The chasing crowd were close; he could hear their angry shouts and threats. As he ran, he made his metal hand turn into a claw and managed to hook it below the man's body through the loop of rope. Then Jake tripped and was dragged along too, his feet making grooves in the grass.

'Up, up, up!' shouted Billy and, as Charlotte pulled hard on a lever that let the elevators harness the wind, Jake and the unconscious man rose in the air just out of reach of the braying mob.

'I don't fink I've got the strength to wind 'em back up again,' shouted Billy.

'Allow me.' It was Oliver. 'Has Jakey-boy gone for a spot of sightseeing?' Oliver braced himself against the door and started to rewind the rope. It was on a ratchet, so there was no danger of Jake and the stranger slipping back down if he let go and took a rest. Eventually, Oliver and Billy hauled the two men aboard. Jake lay on the floor, panting with exhaustion. Their new passenger gradually regained consciousness and began to groan.

'Shut the door,' Oliver said to Billy, 'You don't want him to roll out after all that effort, and Charlotte, allow me to congratulate you on a fine bit of flying.' Charlotte's only response was to utter:

'Why, he's black!'

CHAPTER SEVEN

'Yes, I am black,' said the man, getting to his feet. Then, sensing the movement of the airship, he rushed to the window, amazed that he was so far above the ground. 'Does that mean you will throw me out of the door?'

'No, I'm sorry,' said Charlotte flustered, 'I don't know why I said that. Why were they chasing you?' The man paused before he answered.

'I am a slave. I ran away. Does that mean you will hand me back?'

'Why no! Of course not. But slavery was abolished in the 1830s. How can you be a slave?'

'I was taken from Africa and sold as a slave in America. I came to this country with my master. There are many like me. You might not call us slaves anymore, but we are. Nothing in my life changed when I came here. I still have to work; if I don't, I am beaten. I am not fed well and I don't receive wages. I do not have the freedom to do what I want or go where I like, even when I have finished the day's work. Call it what you want, but that is the life of a slave.'

'Goodness!' murmured Charlotte, 'But what made you run away now? Did something happen?

'I was working in the garden outside the big house, pulling up weeds below an open window. I couldn't help overhearing what they were saying inside. The master and another man were planning a trip to capture more of my people, more slaves, and sell them directly to the Americans.'

'But, but, that's against the law!' gasped Charlotte.

'I don't know about that; there are some laws for people like you and others for people like me. Anyway, a red mist came over me as I remembered my capture, and I threw down my spade.' He started to chuckle, 'Actually, I threw it through the window.'

'That's my man!' cried Oliver.

'And I started to run. I made such a noise because I didn't throw my spade through the open part of the window - I broke the glass.'

'Hah, hah,' laughed Oliver, 'Sometimes, there is a time for strategy, and sometimes there is a time for action. If you had crept away quietly, we would not have found you. Welcome aboard, my man. What is your name?'

'My English name is Joshua.'

'What is the name of this Master of yours?' asked Jake.

'His name is Robert Fotheringay.' There was a pause before Charlotte spoke.

'He's my Uncle,' she whispered.

Several regulars took one look inside The Rat and Whippet and decided to find another pub. Menacing groups of men, all wearing the tell-tale items of dress that indicated they were gang members, were keeping a wary eye on each other. Inside the snug, a small room at the back of the pub, the only occupants were three men sitting around a table. They were leaders of the gangs that controlled the underworld in most of London.

'You may have an inkling about why I called this meeting,' said Crusty Jack from the Black Feathers.

'I have, but go on,' replied Whisky Pete, who led The Wild Boys.

'My boys took some persuading to come to The Rookery, but I will hear what you have to say,' said Jungle from the Golden-Lane gang.

'I'll come straight to the point,' continued Crusty Jack, 'These are strange times, and I think they will get stranger. It started with this business of the horses, and I reckon things will take a turn. I can't say if it will be a turn for the better or a turn for the worse, but I'll tell you this: when the time comes, if there is an opening, we have to be ready to step into it. And that means we can't be doing with fighting each other or watching our backs. If the opportunity arises, we've got to move quickly and go for the jugular.'

'So, who are our targets?' asked Whisky Pete.

'I've thought about that,' replied Crusty Jack. He placed a hand-written list on the table. 'When we rise up, and I'm sure that day will come sooner rather than later, these people should receive a swift, sudden and violent visitation from your boys.'

'It will be our turn to take a bite of the cherry,' said

Jungle, nodding in approval.

'Cherry-bite,' said Crusty Jack. 'Let that be our signal.'

'Cherry-bite,' they all repeated.

'I hope you don't mind us having afternoon tea at home instead of the West End,' said Arabella, 'Only getting around is proving so frightfully difficult!'

'No, no, dear. It's certainly all very puzzling,' said Edward.

'What is, dear? The horses all dying?'

'No, I mean this business with Fotheringay's. You would think that if his daughter were missing, he would have at least told the Bow Street Runners, but they were unaware of the situation and were not actively searching for her. The same goes for the fellow with the hook for a hand.'

'A hook! How perfectly dreadful. Have you not considered that she does not want anyone to find her? Maybe they are lovers.'

'It's possible, but anyone in authority I ask puts up a wall of silence. I've spoken to soldiers who told me they are looking for a chap with a hook, but they do not seem to know why.'

'I'll speak to my father,' said Arabella, 'He still has great influence. Now, more tea, Edward?'

'Please ask him if the name Tiberius means anything to him.'

'Surely he was a Roman Emperor?'

'True, but one of Fotheringay's designers mentioned the name and then clamped his mouth shut as though he had said too much, and I couldn't get any more out of him.'

'An update, Hastings.' Fotheringay looked at the man in charge of locating Jake Moss, otherwise known as Hooky. He had permitted Hastings to leave his bowler hat on. Fotheringay did not particularly care to see the man's scalp - shaved, stitched and stained yellow with iodine, and Hastings certainly did not want other workers to see the damage caused by a lowly cleaner.

'It's gone cold, Sir. We don't think they are in The Rookery. They almost certainly left through the factory. If I had been at the door, I wouldn't have fallen for such a trick and left my post. Either they have another girl with them, or it was your daughter in disguise that helped them.'

'I've washed my hands of her. Find her if you can, and we shall lock her away where she can do no more harm, but most importantly, find this Hooky; find out what he knows and who he's told and then silence him. For good!'

'Don't you worry about that, Sir. I'll find him if it's the last thing I ever do! My revenge will be sweet…and brutal!'

'I hate this job,' complained Corporal Jones, 'I'd much rather be out on the battlefield fighting the French, or the Germans or the Turks.'

'Don't forget the Russians,' said Private Smith.

'Yeh, I hate them too, but not half as much as I hate guard duty outside the flaming Rookery! Animals they are. Look at them now. What are they up to? They can't be no more than ten, and they keep running up shouting 'Cherry-bite, cherry-bite.''

'I ask you, what does that even mean?' asked Smith.

'Hold up, look lively. What's going on 'ere?' The

soldiers watched a line of men wearing bowler hats with rook feathers tucked into the brim advance slowly towards the gate from within The Rookery and stop around ten feet away. Some of the men were carrying sledgehammers and they pounded them in unison on the ground.

'What the...? Sarge, you better get out here! Quick!' shouted the corporal from the small building that acted as their garrison when they were on guard duty. Ten men tumbled out of the door. They shouldered their rifles and pointed them at the gang.

'Go back,' shouted the sergeant.

'I was just going to say the same thing to you,' replied Crusty Jack with a throaty laugh.

'Go back, or we shoot. I'll count to three. One...Two...' Before the sergeant could say 'three', a crashing blow came down on the back of each soldier's head. Their tour of duty was over.

'Didn't they teach you about rearguard actions in that army of yours?' sneered Whisky Pete. The air filled with screaming from women who happened to be passing, and cheering from the young boys within The Rookery. Meanwhile, the Black Feathers beat their sledgehammers rhythmically against the hinges of the metal gates until, eventually, the barrier between The Rookery and the rest of London crashed to the ground. Immediately the street urchins streamed out. Most of them had never left The Rookery before and the moment felt delicious. Flagons of ale were fetched and the united gang members retired to the garrison house to celebrate their quick and savage victory.

'I reckon we've got about thirty minutes before word gets back,' said Crusty Jack. 'We know the route they will take to get here. They are creatures of habit, and of course, they will be on foot. They are going to encounter the Golden-Lane gang on the way. They won't be expecting that. I'll be surprised if they make it this far for a showdown with us. They won't have experienced the way we fight before. None of that marching along in a thin red line in full view of the enemy. The Golden-Lane gang will be in and out of a dozen different alleyways. If the soldiers give chase, they will be finished. If they don't, they will pick them off one by one. I predict they will turn tail, run back home and decide The Rookery ain't worth defending. Come on, let's drag those gates out of the way. They, my friends, are a thing of the past.'

'Incredible!' said Edward to his wife, Arabella. 'Parts of London are descending into chaos and the politicians seem oblivious to it all. They only care about scoring points off each other.'

'Do be careful, dear, about where you go.' Edward nodded; he hadn't told her about his visits to The Rookery.

'Arabella, was your father able to throw any light on the other mystery -not the ineptitude or perhaps ambivalence of the members of parliament - but about Fotheringay, Tiberius and the man with the hook?'

'No, he was not. In fact, he got very cross, and he was quite firm about saying that you must not pursue this matter any further.' Edward opened his mouth to protest but then shut it again. He knew better than to argue with his wife. It would be wiser to follow the course he believed right, quietly and without attracting attention.

'More tea, dear,' he murmured. What was odd was that The Times had taken the same tack as Arabella's father. The editor was sending him out of town to investigate a rural story, and Edward thought it was a pretext for getting him out of the way. Surely a story about a theft from a farmhouse couldn't be as important as reporting the troubles on their own doorstep?

The Cavalry Club, Mayfair.

'The situation has worsened ten-fold since we last met,' said Bellings.

'I heard about the skirmish at the gates to The Rookery,' replied Fotheringay.

'It wasn't just in that district. The regiment we sent as reinforcements was decimated. We've had to withdraw. I can't spare the manpower to close off The Rookery. The inhabitants poured out like rats from a sewer. There is no more I can do. We are facing insurrection throughout the city. We have to retreat and regroup. It's not as though we are getting any help from the Government. These gangs - they don't fight fair!'

'I have some good news,' said Fotheringay, holding up his glass of claret to admire its colour. 'We have started building our prototype of Tiberius, and can begin tests in the next few days.'

'And the spy? Have you found him?'

'Not yet, but we will. After all, he can't have disappeared into thin air!'

CHAPTER EIGHT

'Stone the crows! There's anuvver one,' said Billy,' spotting a dead horse below. A red kite circled the field in search of carrion, but the crows had got there first. A single crow gave chase to the large winged scavenger, driving it away. The kite soared higher and higher before giving up and heading south.

'Have any of you seen any horses alive?' asked Jake. Everyone shook their heads, everyone, that is, except for Oliver, who was fast asleep again. It was a slumber fortified by a little wine, but hopefully, he would sleep it off before it was his turn to take over the controls from Charlotte.

'All the horses on the estate died,' said Joshua. 'They were trying to buy oxen to pull the carts, but there are not enough of them for sale, and now they are very, very expensive because of the demand.'

"Ave a butchers!' cried Billy. They were passing over the outskirts of a city. Below them the roads leading towards open countryside were thronged with hundreds of people.

'Where are they going?' wondered Charlotte.

'I don't know, but I hope they are not going to the same place we're going. I was hoping for a little peace and quiet,' replied Jake.

'Where are we going?' asked Joshua.

'I can tell you that.' Oliver was awake at last. 'We are going to a remote Scottish Island called Foula, and don't worry, there will be plenty of peace and quiet. That is, if you don't count the racket the seagulls make.' Oliver peered out of the window. 'And as for them, I have a theory. I felt something ugly in the air before we left London, and I wouldn't be surprised if that same undercurrent of disorder replicated itself in every major city. I reckon those people originally came from the countryside and went to the city in search of work but are now fleeing back to the world they once knew, somewhere where they will feel safe.'

'Strange times and new beginnings for all of us,' mused Jake. 'Strange times indeed!'

Edward had mixed emotions. On the one hand, he was disgruntled because he felt his editor had sent him away from London to keep him out of the way. Given the amount of unrest in the Capital, anything he wrote would be inconsequential. On the other hand and on a positive note, Edward was excited at the opportunity of travelling on a train. Tickets were hard to come by, but the editor had pulled a few strings, and now he was sitting in an open-topped, third-class carriage bearing the distinctive plum and cream livery of the London and North Western Railway. A whistle blew and, in a cloud of steam, the engine slowly pulled away from Euston Station and Edward's journey north began.

The train's final destination was Birmingham, but Edward wasn't going that far. He alighted at Market Bashford.

'Manor House Farm, you say. That would be in that direction,' said the Station Master, pointing to the road. 'Take you maybe an hour to walk. No cabs anymore.' After checking the times of the return trains, Edward thanked him and started to walk. An hour later, he knocked on the door of a grand limestone building. Parts of Manor House Farm were medieval in origin, but there was also evidence of a new wing under construction - a sign that this was a profitable business.

'Can I help you?' asked the elderly servant who answered the door.

'My name is Edward Ramsey. I have an appointment to meet James Medstone, the estate manager.'

'Come in; you are expected.' The servant took Edward to a reception room. Edward thought of himself as a modern-thinking, humanitarian and intellectual person. James Medstone, a brusque man who clearly would rather have been somewhere else, displayed the opposite of all those qualities.

'Well, what do you expect of those darkies? I wouldn't have let him anywhere near the house if I'd been here.'

'So you weren't actually present when the incident occurred,' suggested Edward.

'No, I was still walking back from the market. If you ask me, you should keep them working in the fields, but some bright spark had the idea of letting him work in the gardens.'

'And you say he stole a silver candlestick,' asked Edward, consulting his notes.

'That's right; the beggar wants hanging!' Medstone gritted his teeth and folded his arms. As far as he was concerned, the interview was over.

'As it took me such a long time to get here, would it be possible to talk to someone who took part in the chase?'

'Well, I don't know about that. I suppose you could speak to Percy, the head groom. He was there.' Edward was led outside into a courtyard where he waited whilst Medstone went to find Percy. When he returned he was accompanied by his groom. The two were deep in conversation. Then, to Medstone's annoyance, he was called away by a servant, who had brought a message from the master of the house, leaving Edward to talk to Percy alone. The groom seemed a little nervous at first and recounted the incident in very similar terms to those outlined by James Medstone.

'I'm interested to hear about the chase,' said Edward. 'All Mr Medstone said was that the thief ran away and several people chased him, but he escaped.' Percy relaxed a little now.

'Oh, it was very exciting, We was a-running and a-hollering. It was like a fox hunt, only more fun. But he's a big strong brute of a man is Joshua, and we weren't catching him until he slipped and hit his head and it knocked him out cold. Then, would you believe it, this airship appeared out of nowhere.'

'An airship! Mr Medstone never mentioned an airship!'

'Well, he weren't there, were he? 'It had a bolt of lightning painted on the side. Anyway, I thought, 'We've got 'im,' but this fellow arrived on a rope from the sky, fastened it around Joshua, and hauled him up into the airship, still unconscious.'

'And was he still holding onto the candlestick?'

'Erm, he must have been 'cause it weren't there afterwards. I was too busy looking at the other fellow. I thought he was going to get left behind, only he had this metal hand, and he hooked it onto the rope, and up he went a-dangling and a-spinning.'

'What?' exclaimed Edward excitedly. 'He had a hook for a hand?'

'That's right.'

'Which way did they go?'

'North.'

'Ain't England a big place?' chirped Billy.

'The world is a big place. We are a long way from Africa,' replied Joshua.

'I think you will find that we are flying over Scotland right now,' said Oliver.

'This place we are going to, Foula,' said Jake, 'I don't suppose there is a foundry there or somewhere that sells parts for clockwork machines, is there?'

'No, nothing like that. Just a part-time blacksmith. Why do you ask?'

'I'm certain I can improve your clockwork drive. Then Billy wouldn't have to do so much winding.'

'I'm all for that!' yelled Billy.

'But I need some more parts. Cogs mostly.'

'Interesting. As it happens, we are not too far from Edinburgh, where all of the parts for my motor drive came from. We could make a little detour. I have a taste for some

Highland malt whisky in any case. Charlotte, we should reach a river soon. When we do, follow it around to the west, and it will lead us to Edinburgh.

'Let me look at you all,' said Oliver shortly before the airship reached Edinburgh. 'Jake and Charlotte - you look good, but Joshua, you look like a farm labourer.'

'That's because that is what I was!'

'Exactly. Pull out that trunk and let's see if there is anything that will fit you.' Joshua dragged a large leather trunk into the centre of the cabin. Oliver fished inside it, pulled out some knee-length boots, and handed them to Joshua. 'Will these fit?'

'A little tight, but better than my old farm boots.'

'I'll get you some more as soon as I can. How about this?' Oliver unfurled a long tartan cloak. 'It was a present from a clansman. I think it will be received very well here in Edinburgh.' Joshua wrapped it around himself. 'There! You look like a prince!' said Oliver, nodding in approval. 'Billy, I don't have much that will fit you. Try this! It's too small for me.' He flung a top hat in Billy's direction. Billy beamed, not at all worried that the hat was was at least two sizes too big and kept sliding down and covering his eyes. 'And of course,' continued Oliver. 'How could I forget? I have a habit of leaving these in hostelries throughout the land. So I keep lots of spares.'

Jake smiled, as he could well imagine the condition that Oliver got into in the pubs he visited, but he grinned from ear to ear when Oliver handed out a pair of flying goggles to every member of his crew.

'Now we look the part,' said Oliver. 'Charlotte, the castle is ahead. Slow down and prepare to dock. I need someone to shimmy down a rope to tie her rear to an iron hoop, if you'll pardon my expression.'

'I am happy to do that, I was a sailor before I was a slave,' said Joshua.

"It was a day like no other, and just what the beleaguered Royal city of Edinburgh needed," wrote Hamish McWorter later for 'The Scotsman.' He described the scene as the airship glided into view and hovered over the castle walls. Then Joshua, his tartan cloak flying in the wind, slid down a rope to the ground. He secured the airship and stood like a statue so the children could gather around him. Many of them had never seen a black man and were in awe of this tartan-clad giant. Next Oliver unfurled a rope ladder, and the remaining crew members descended to the cheering crowd. Oliver gave some coins to a group of young men and asked them to 'mind' his airship and, making sure they wouldn't immediately disappear to the nearest pub; he promised to double that amount when he returned. Then, the crew formed into a 'V', with Oliver at the front and, proudly wearing their goggles, they marched into town, surrounded by whooping and laughing children.

'Aye, things have been bad since all the horses died,' complained Bruce Robertson, the supplier of clockwork parts. 'The people of Edinburgh feel like the English have forgotten them. There is a lot of talk about declaring independence. My great-grandfather died at the Battle of Culloden. A thousand highlanders died that day. It has not been forgotten. The nationalists aren't the only ones in search of power. The razor gangs have taken over Edinburgh, Glasgow and Aberdeen.' As if on cue, the doors swung open, and two tough-looking youths swaggered in.

'We hae come tae collect a wee package,' said one. Oliver's hand went to his sword stick, but Bruce shot him a warning glance and handed over a packet. Its size suggested that it contained money. After the gang members had left the shop, sharing at a joke, no doubt at the expense of Bruce and the airship crew, Bruce placed a warning hand on Oliver's arm.

'I know you could take those two little runts with one hand behind your back, but it would be no good. You can't stay here to protect me all the time, and they would soon be back in force demanding even more protection money.'

'But who are they protecting you from?' asked Charlotte innocently.

'From themselves,' explained Bruce. 'There have been several cases of shops belonging to owners who refused to pay being burnt to the ground. Whole terraces caught fire in a couple of cases because there were no horses to pull the fire engines. Anyway,' he said, turning to Jake. I believe you are looking for cogs and springs and the like. You've come to the right place. Follow me.'

Jake couldn't believe his eyes. He felt like a five-year-old in a sweetshop, only this time, there was drawer upon drawer of parts for clockwork motors, everything that he could ever want. As well as cogs for the airship improvements, Oliver had said he could buy some other items that might come in useful in the future.

'Yes, of course, have a free hand,' Oliver had said, chuckling to himself as he, Joshua and Billy left the shop. Oliver knew that Jake had ideas about making another prosthetic hand. Not for cosmetic reasons, his plan this time was to build a hand that would serve as a tool and incorporate clockwork drills, pliers and spanners. When Jake had finished choosing his cogs and spindles, they were loaded onto a handcart to be collected later, and then he and Charlotte took a leisurely walk to the hotel where they had agreed to meet the others. They were all looking forward to a hot meal. A procession of children followed them.

'I feel like I'm a King, and you are my Queen,' said Jake proudly.

'So very high-handed to claim me as your Queen without first having wooed me,' laughed Charlotte.

'Oh no!' replied Jake, blushing, 'I didn't mean it like that; I meant that I feel special for the first time in my life.'

'I'm only teasing. I know we come from different backgrounds, but I feel the same as you. Up to now, I've always been just somebody's daughter. The family name meant more than my personal identity, and I felt I was just being bred to marry into another wealthy family and make more money for the...the Fotheringays.' She couldn't help pausing - she was ashamed of her own family name. 'But now, these children are following me because of who I am.' Charlotte paused again and placed the goggles that had been lying loosely around her neck over her eyes and with a smile, she looked at Jake: 'It was me who flew an airship into Edinburgh, and you, Jake, are going to make her fly even better.'

The meal at the hotel was a great success.

'Copy me,' whispered Charlotte to Jake, Joshua and Billy as they stared in confusion at the array of cutlery. Oliver didn't seem to care. As he downed his third glass of wine, Charlotte wondered how many whiskies he had consumed before making his selection at 'The House of Malt.'

'I'm looking forward to you showing me how to take off in the airship,' she whispered to Oliver, in an attempt to slow down his intake. He would have to remain sober enough until then - or, at the very least, awake! The others were on their best behaviour - it was the finest meal they had ever eaten. As for Charlotte, although she was used to fine dining, she had never enjoyed a dinner as much as this one.

Bruce's son pushed a handcart to the airship, where Oliver, Charlotte, Jake, Billy and Joshua were already assembled and waving to the cheering crowds. A photographer who had been waiting all afternoon for this moment focussed his large glass plate camera and captured the moment. All five travellers were wearing new clothes. Charlotte had found a suit in a hunting shop, consisting of a long jacket gathered at the waist with a leather belt and, more importantly, and unusually for women - trousers. If she was going to spend time climbing up and down rope ladders in the future, she did not want people looking up her skirt! Joshua had well-fitting boots and a velvet jerkin and breeches that matched his tartan cloak. Jake had chosen a leather outfit as he thought it would be practical, and Billy seemed to be wearing every colour under the sun. He had truly left his foggy, grey, London riverbank life behind him. One by one, the crew climbed the ladder, leaving Joshua on the ground to untie the airship. As Charlotte began the ascent, Joshua gripped the rope between his new boots, rose in the air and waved to the excited crowds before shinning expertly up to the gondola.

'So, you said to head north to these coordinates?' Charlotte asked Oliver. When she glanced over her shoulder, he was already snoring.

Joshua

I feel like I'm driftwood. Like I'm a branch torn from a tree in a storm and now floating on the ocean. Neither part of the sea nor part of the land. I roll up the sand with the waves, and then the tide takes me out again.

I was nineteen when they took me from Africa. I cannot describe the nightmare of that journey in the hold of the slaver's ship. If I close my eyes, I can still see the rats feasting on countrymen who did not survive the journey. Because I was big for my age, I always had to carry the dead up to the deck and throw them overboard. It seemed a release for them, and there was many a time when I considered following them into the sea, but I felt life couldn't get any worse, so I resisted.

Life improved when we got to America, but only in comparison with my time on the ship. I had been used to working hard, but now my labour was to make others rich, not me. I picked cotton in the South for years, and then I was sold to a man who exported cotton to Great Britain, which was how I ended up coming to England.

Now I am glad I never jumped into the waves all those years ago. I may be hunted, but I am free. I may not be the African that I once was, I have seen too much to go back to the simplicity of my old life there, but now I feel I am a member of a new tribe and have a future that I can determine for myself.

CHAPTER NINE

Edward was excited. He rushed into the editor's office to tell him the news about finding the trail of the man with the hook, but before he could get his words out, the editor snapped at him.

'What took you so long?'

'Erm, erm,' stammered Edward, 'It takes a long time getting anywhere these days.'

'I expected you hours ago; get yourself down to the House of Commons immediately. I've been hearing rumours about something important. You need to be there!'

'But, but, I wanted to tell you about the man with the hook. Hooky.'

'I thought I made myself perfectly clear!' shouted the

editor, 'That matter is closed. Fotheringay has his own investigators and our proprietors have instructed us to leave it in their hands. Now get out of my sight!'

Edward sidled miserably into the Strangers Gallery in the Houses of Parliament. The editor couldn't have been the only one to have heard rumours because it was packed to the rafters.

Afterwards, Edward reflected that he was glad he had hurried to get there. He was sure his editor would have sacked him if he had missed the events that ensued soon after his arrival. The politicians were debating whether they should reduce the tax on imported corn, given the current food shortages. As most of the politicians were also landowners, they had a vested interest in keeping things as they were, so the debate wasn't making much progress. Suddenly, the doors burst open, accompanied by a gasp of horror from the seated politicians, and around twenty armed soldiers led by Field Marshal Bellings marched down the central aisle. Bellings went straight to the table at the head of the chamber and seized the mace, the symbol of royal authority.

'Order, order!' shouted the Speaker of the House, trying in vain to regain authority. Soldiers surrounded the Field Marshal, and no one appeared willing to try and retrieve the mace.

'Silence!' shouted a soldier in a voice that would project to the back of a parade ground. The stunned politicians obeyed him. Then Field Marshal Bellings spoke:

'The country is in crisis. We cannot sit back and let our fair land decline further. I wish to inform you that Great Britain is under Martial Law from this point onwards. Gentlemen, I suggest you return to your constituencies.' He then looked up to where Edward and the other spectators were seated. 'In the national interest, The Strangers Gallery will be closed until further notice. Please leave forthwith!'

'The death of democracy,' Edward wrote in his notebook before a soldier forced him to leave his seat.

Edward rushed back to the office to file his report. There was little worthwhile for him to do in the office afterwards, so despite his editor's earlier warning, he decided to visit Fotheringay's Steam Works.

'So, they have their own investigators, do they?' he thought, 'Maybe we could share information.' Edward was shown to a small office to wait. He examined a map of London on the wall; he presumed the coloured pins indicated where the investigators had searched for the young man with the hook.

If Edward had found the estate manager at Manor House Farm unpleasant, Hastings, who now blustered into the office, was even more disagreeable.

'What's all this? I haven't got time to talk to the newspapers. I'm a busy man!'

'Erm, it's about the man with a hook,' began Edward.

'You have been told to keep your nose out! We've got the matter covered. We're searching every inch of London. He won't get far,' said Hastings, jabbing his finger at the map. 'Now, I bid you good day. I have work to do.'

'But, but, he already has got far. I've spoken to someone who has seen him. Two days ago, he was passing over Market Bashford in an airship with a lightning bolt painted on the side, heading North.'

'What!' exclaimed Hastings, 'How did he get a ride in an airship? Never mind. Thank you for the information, Mr Romsey.'

'Actually, it's Ramsey.'

'And is that the full extent of your knowledge, Mr

Romsey?'

'Ramsey. Yes, it is. I was hoping that we could pool our knowledge and work together.'

'No, that won't be possible, Mr Romsey. We have our ways and means and don't want any hangers-on. We'll catch him, bring him to book, and mark my words; he'll be one for the gallows. Good day, Mr Romsey. See yourself out.'

Edward sat for a moment, stunned by the ferocity of the man. Then he realised there was one more question he needed to ask. He noticed a young girl scrubbing the floor on her hands and knees.

'Excuse me,' he said, 'This young man with the hook who has disappeared - I don't suppose you know his real name?'

'Well, I do actually, Mister, 'Cause he once told me he hated being called 'Hooky'. His name is Jake Moss.'

'So, Jake Moss,' thought Edward as he walked home, 'I don't know if I have done the right thing in telling Hastings about you. So I'll just have to find you first.'

'At last!' breathed Charlotte. Directly below them was a scattering of islands. 'We must have travelled a hundred miles since mainland Scotland slipped behind us. I was beginning to worry that we had got our calculations wrong and we were heading for the North Pole!'

'If we were, it would have been my fault,' replied Jake. 'I had the responsibility for reading this beautiful sextant. Don't you just love the engineering that has gone into making this? And there's the evidence below. We must be cleverer than we thought!'

'Head for the tiny island to the west of the main group; that's Foula,' said Oliver, coming to the helm. 'It's Scotland, but we are actually closer to Norway than to Edinburgh. When we arrive, I want you to lower her until you are just below the level of the cliffs. It will be scary the first time you do it, Charlotte. The cliffs are impressive - the second highest in Britain - and you will feel you are flying straight into a sheer wall of sandstone, but there is a beacon on top of the cliff. Directly below it is a fissure in the rock - an airship-shaped crack. But, and it's a big but, it runs diagonally, so once you get her nose in, you have to pause and swing her tail round, then glide in.'

'Oh! It sounds very tricky. Don't you think you should take over?'

'No. I'm sure you will rise to the challenge. Don't panic, and keep a gentle touch - just like you have been doing so far. I must warn you though; it will be windy. It always is on Foula.' With her heart in her mouth, Charlotte steered the airship towards the beacon. She didn't see the opening in the cliffs until the last moment because it was hidden from the open sea. Charlotte turned the helm to port whilst putting the engines into reverse to slow the airship down, and pulled on a lever to move the stern to starboard. At first, her touch was too heavy, and the tail swung around further than she intended. She gave an involuntary scream, but remembering Oliver's, 'Don't panic,' she eased back on the controls. The airship bounced gently against the sides of the crevice before steadying into a more central position.

'That's my girl,' laughed Oliver. Charlotte didn't know if he was saying it to the airship or her. 'Flip the propellers; you need to descend about twenty feet,' he continued calmly. 'There! See a large shiny ring fixed into the side of the cliff? Head for that. I'll be ready with the mounting clip.'

Moments later, Charlotte sank down into a chair. Her heart was still racing. She had done it! It wasn't perfect, but she had done it.

'Excellent!' beamed Oliver, 'You should have seen me the first time I tried it. I was bouncing off the sides like a rubber ball. It's a good spot, though, because the cliff shelters us from the wind and hides us from passing ships.'

'I don't have to climb down there, do I?' said Joshua with concern, looking at the sea, raging and crashing against the rocks below.

'No! We can tether the airship to the rockface through the windows, and there is a ladder fixed to the cliff in line with the door - we will be going up, not down. I hope none of you is afraid of heights. If you are, what are you doing in an airship?'

No one had vertigo, although they all heeded Oliver's advice and avoided looking down. There then followed an hour's walk across a green but treeless, windswept moor.

'You've took us to the bleedin' edge of the world!' gasped Billy. There could be nowhere that would contrast so completely with the world he knew. No roads or paths, no people and a constant biting wind. 'Why here?'

'I feel safe here,' replied Oliver, 'The Shetland islands are as remote as you can get. Who could find us here?'

They passed a few cottages but didn't see a soul, and then clustering close to the coast, they saw more buildings.

'Ere, there's a village down there,' exclaimed Billy, pointing.

'That, my friend, is Ham, and it is the only town on this little island,' replied Oliver.

'But it's tiny!' said Billy.

'It's a tiny island, maybe only five square miles. There can't be more than two hundred people living here.'

'There must have been a hundred people living down my alley in The Rookery,' laughed Jake.

'Anyway, we have reached our destination. People call this house - or should I say 'Hoose'? - The Haa.' They stood before an unprepossessing square building with roughcast walls and a large and incongruous, castellated sandstone porch. 'Needless to say, no one is expecting us. Follow me.' Oliver strode up to the front door, knocked on it loudly, tried the handle, opened the door and went in. A little nervously, the others followed, knowing Oliver was inclined to be unpredictable. Was this what one did in Foula? Just walked into people's houses without being invited in? Oliver hollered up the stairs, but the house was clearly empty. 'The kitchen is through here. Let's make a cup of tea.'

A little later, as they sat around a large farmhouse table drinking tea, Charlotte asked:

'So, I imagine you know the owner of this house?' Before Oliver could answer, there was a voice at the door.

'Oh aye, and I know Oliver very well indeed.' They all looked to see who had spoken. A man holding an axe stood in the doorway; he was the spitting image of Oliver.

'Allow me to introduce my older brother, although only by four minutes. My friends, this is Alexander Moon, The Laird of Foula.'

'Erm…How can I put this? Are you alike in every way?' asked Charlotte.

'Chalk and cheese,' replied Alexander.

Charlotte breathed an audible sigh of relief.

'Only, I don't think I have room for two men like Oliver Moon in my life,' she continued.

That broke the ice, and everyone laughed.

'Is this where you was brought up?' asked Billy,

looking first at Oliver and then at Alexander, 'You don't sound very Scottish, well, not like them people in Edinburgh.'

'Many of the locals here speak another language, more like Norwegian. It's called Norn, but Oliver and I went to school and University in England,' replied Alexander. 'Our father was the Laird, but he was largely absent, preferring the comfort of a large country house in Yorkshire, although we sometimes came here for holidays. After university, Oliver joined the army; then, after our parents died, I came to live here. I tried the high life in London but needed somewhere to live where I could think.'

'My brother is a poet,' explained Oliver.

'And my brother occasionally needs somewhere to sober up,' laughed Alexander.

Over the next few weeks, life settled into a pattern, and everyone got something different out of Foula.

'Welcome to my new workshop,' said Jake to Charlotte, who had come to the outbuilding to see what was keeping him so busy.

'I can see you've arranged all the cogs you bought in Edinburgh in size order,' laughed Charlotte, 'Do you remember that first morning when we were looking for one that had rolled off the table in the hotel room?'

'Yes, doesn't that seem a long time ago? A lifetime ago!'

'What a lot of drawings!'

'They are different configurations for the airship's winding mechanism.'

'So they are. Oliver mentioned that he had introduced you to the only blacksmith on the island.'

'Yes, his name is Jed. I can't tell you how upset I was when I realised I had miscalculated and hadn't bought enough spindles, but Jed is happy to pass on his skills and has taught me how to make more. So, when I'm not in this dark outbuilding, I'm in another dark room, lit by the fire and sparks from a furnace and beating metal into shape on an ancient anvil. I'll be ready soon to start modifying the airship'

'What do you want to do with yourself, Billy?' Alexander had asked.

'Yer might fink it's daft, but Mr Moon took us to a posh 'otel for a nosh and I ain't tasted nuffink like it afore. There was flavours wot proper took the top of me 'ead off. I wanna learn 'ow to cook.'

'Hah, well, you won't learn anything from me, I lead a simple life, but there is a young lady on the island, Mary. She used to work in the kitchen of a fancy restaurant in Edinburgh; she returned to look after her sick mother but I dare say she could show you a thing or two. You could give her a hand around the place.' From then on, the others did not see a lot of Billy, but after a while, thanks to an extra allowance that Oliver gave Mary to buy more provisions, Billy would often appear in the evenings with a delicious stew or an apple pie he had made.

For a few days, Joshua did nothing. Throughout his life as a slave, he had been forced to work every day and now it was time to do the exact opposite. However, he eventually became restless and sought out Alexander.

'I need to do something. My muscles will get flabby.

Perhaps I could chop some wood for you?'

'I'm afraid there aren't many trees on Foula. We burn peat here to heat our houses and cook with. As it happens, there has been a call to help cut peat for one of the widows on the island. You can volunteer for that. It's certainly hard work.'

'Sure! I'm ready for that. I will cut more peat than any man has ever cut before. I will make a mountain of peat. I have one question. What is peat?'

'Ha ha! It's a layer under the turf - decayed vegetation from thousands of years ago. You will have to dig up slabs and lay them out to dry. Oh! And watch out for the Bonxies'

'What are they?'

'They're seabirds, Great Skuas; if you dig too close to their nest, you had better duck because they will dive at your head and their beaks are fearful sharp! '

Oliver stared at the half-full bottle of whisky he had brought from the airship. His whole body was shaking, but he wouldn't give in and reach for the bottle.

'When was the last time you spent a day without alcohol passing your lips?' asked his brother. Oliver simply shook his head. Too long ago to remember!

'You were crying out in your sleep again last night.'

'Ah! I've not been sleeping well lately. It's a struggle.'

'Do you think the clothes will fit you?' asked Alexander as he walked with Charlotte across the moor.

'It really doesn't matter,' replied Charlotte, 'I've always enjoyed needlework, so I'm sure I can adapt them to suit my new life.'

'Elsie's daughters certainly won't want them back now they have started a new life in America.'

'My days of wearing frills, buttons and bows are over. I see them as a symbol of the life I've walked away from, or rather flown away from!'

'I get your point. I can't say I would relish going back to society life in London. I'm happier in my tweed jacket and corduroy breeches.'

'Another way you are so different from Oliver,' laughed Charlotte.

'Aye, that's true. Oliver always did like a uniform, and now he gets to create his own. Maybe there is something deeper behind it, as though the clothes are a disguise that he hides behind and...' Alexander broke off because Charlotte had let out a squeal - half shock, half excitement. As they came out from behind a big craggy rock, there, running as free as the wind, was a herd of wild Shetland ponies!

'Look, and enjoy this moment,' said Alexander, 'We'll talk more about it this evening.'

'I'm glad you are all here. Now we have eaten Billy's delicious pie, I have something important to say,' said Alexander. 'I called a meeting with everyone on the island a few weeks ago and we made a decision. We will not tell anyone about our ponies and neither should you. We know what has happened to the horses on the mainland. Not just in Great Britain but all over the world. Whether this killer horse flu is transmitted by contact with humans or blown on the wind, we just don't know. The ponies have lived in these Isles for four thousand years; they don't need us to survive, so we will let them be. We won't go near them and will fight anybody who tries to steal them.' Oliver slammed his fist down on the table.

'And we will fight alongside you, brother!'

CHAPTER TEN

It was shortly after dawn and already, in Westminster, a full cabinet meeting was in progress. Field Marshal Bellings surveyed the Generals seated around the long table. He trusted them implicitly. He had sent army officers who didn't support the military coup on indefinite 'gardening leave'. General Truscott was the first to give his report.

'We have assumed control of all railways in the country. Of course, the owners will be compensated, but we must be able to transport troops to quell any unrest. It means we can still only reach large swathes of the country on foot. Any civilians who wish to travel need express permission from an army committee. We are monitoring the situation on the canals. If there is any indication that supplies - especially of coal - are being held up, we will not hesitate to take control of the waterways. As you know, coal is a vital commodity and is regularly transported by canal.' Another General raised his hand:

'Can I interject, Sir? There are worrying reports that coal supplies are dwindling due to the absence of pit ponies. We are seriously eating into the reserves. Without coal, there is no steam; without steam, the trains won't run. I feel strongly that the supply of coal must first serve the needs of the army because, without the army, there will be chaos!'

'I've heard things are pretty chaotic already,' said Field Marshal Bellings. 'Major Blackford, an update on the situation in London, please.'

'Sir, we have strategically withdrawn from certain areas of London to focus the troops on protecting areas of economic importance. There is a cordon of men around Toff Town, where most of the captains of industry live, although many residents have already left London and retreated to their country houses. Many of them are landowners, and food supplies are more stable in the countryside. It creates shortages, of course, if they are keeping livestock for themselves rather than sending it to market, but you can't blame them.'

'Have we enough food to feed the men?' asked the Field Marshal.

'If we have to, we could commandeer supplies, but for the moment, we have contracts with our usual suppliers. We pay more now that prices have rocketed, but it makes sense to keep the relationship with our friends sweet.'

'And the general public?'

'Life is undoubtedly harder for them. At some point, we will have to step in because they are more likely to pay protection money to the gangs than to pay their taxes. For now, we have sufficient reserves in the treasury. In the future we may need to arm the tax collectors!'

'I trust the Steam Works is well protected? I have given Fotheringay every assurance.'

'Oh yes, Sir,' nodded Truscott. 'Although we don't anticipate trouble. If the gangs prevented people from going to work, they wouldn't be able to take a cut of their wages!'

Hastings was in a foul mood, and the other members of his 'security team' were taking care not to inflame his anger. He unfurled a map of the Midlands and drew a black cross through the City of Birmingham. Two days had been wasted questioning whether residents had seen an airship. He didn't like their accent, he didn't like their city, and he didn't like the fact that they all said 'No.'

'Back to the railway station, boys,' he growled. 'Let's see if we can get to Nottingham by train; it's a long way to walk.' Fotheringay's links with the new Government ensured Hastings and his men possessed free passes to use the railways. Even so it was going to take a long time to traverse the country. Hastings looked up at the sky as if expecting the airship to cruise past, then, as his rage boiled over, he spat. His men stifled a snigger as they noticed that his spittle had landed on his shoes.

It was a strange start to Edward's day. For the first time since his marriage, he was alone. Arabella had acquiesced to her parent's wishes and had left by train that morning for their country house. Edward's father-in-law had pulled a few strings and managed to get train permits for himself, his wife and his daughter. The other members of his household accompanied the vast quantity of luggage in a goods van, together with a handcart for the long, onward journey from the station. Whilst Edward loved his wife and would miss her, he felt a certain amount of relief now that she was gone because he could get on with his investigation into the disappearance of Jake Moss without interference. Edward walked into the offices of The Times, and the first person he encountered was his editor.

'Ramsey, my office, now!' he barked. Edward knew he was a little late, but he was sure his editor would understand that he had needed to say goodbye to his wife as she left for the country.

'I am sorry I'm late, Sir, but…'

'That's of no consequence,' interrupted his editor, 'I have been informed that you went to The Steam Works and requested an interview to discuss this fellow with the hook. Do you deny it?'

'That's true, Sir, but I had new evidence that…'

'And do you deny that I expressly told you not to pursue this matter?' continued his editor.

'That's true, also, but I…'

'Therefore, I wish to inform you that your position here is untenable, and you are hereby dismissed with immediate effect. Gather your things and go!'

There were very few 'things' to gather. Most important was Edward's fountain pen, now nestling in his inside top pocket and a notebook containing all he knew about the mystery of Jake Moss and his companions. Edward sat on a park bench for twenty minutes, lost in his thoughts. He had failed. His dreams of reaching an audience with insightful and entertaining reports were dashed. How would his wife and her family react? He felt utterly alone. A rhythmical knocking noise grabbed his attention. There in front of him, oblivious to his presence, was a bird, a young thrush, beating a snail shell against a rock. The thrush hadn't perfected the technique; sometimes, it only achieved a glancing blow, and sometimes the snail slipped from its grasp, but the thrush was persistent, and eventually, the shell cracked and the bird was able to enjoy a juicy snail for breakfast.

Edward watched the thrush fly away, and it dawned on him that he had to see his situation as an opportunity. Solving the mystery of the boy with the hook was akin to the bird knocking away at the shell. He had to keep going to find out what was at the heart of this puzzle. He didn't need to tell his wife that he had lost his job just yet. Now he had a free hand, but where to start? He opened his notebook, took his pen from his pocket and stared at the blank page, not knowing what to write. Then he realised he was subconsciously tapping the end of his pen on the notebook, perhaps mimicking the noise that the bird made. Tap tap, tap tap tap, what did it remind him of? Then it came to him. Dot dash, Dot dot dash. It was Morse code. He sprang to his feet:

'Of course! I must use the telegram service,' he cried aloud.

'Welcome to the Electric Telegraph Company,' said the man behind the counter.

'This is a novelty! I've never sent a telegram before,' replied Edward.

'Perhaps I should say, "Welcome to the future", Sir. You have come to the right place. London has several independent companies, but we are the most successful. Perhaps it's still a fairly expensive facility for the general public, but prices will come down. I predict one day, everyone will be able to send messages instantly to each other this way. Posting letters will become a thing of the past.'

Later that day, Edward opened his notebook and surveyed the list detailing his activities. Although he didn't realise it, he had two advantages over Hastings, who was on the same quest. Firstly, he didn't have to visit anywhere personally. Whilst Hastings was sitting on a train for several hours, albeit pleased with himself for having a priority pass, Edward's telegram messages sped along the same route in five minutes. Secondly, Edward had contacts or could easily make new ones. He contacted all the major newspapers across the Midlands, explaining that he was a reporter for The Times researching an article on airships. He hoped that they may have seen his name on parliamentary reports but would not know that he no longer worked for the newspaper. He was in luck. A reporter in Peterborough telegrammed that he had seen the airship, and another in Leeds confirmed that it had passed their way. Edward plotted a course heading North, and the last office he contacted, in Edinburgh, instructed him to look at an issue of "The Scotsman" on the day the airship had docked there.

Edward rushed to the British Museum, where the library kept a copy of all the leading newspapers and there, before his very eyes, was a photograph of the crew of the airship, including the runaway black servant looking resplendent in a tartan cloak and a young lady whom he presumed was Charlotte Fotheringay. Moreover he could just make out the glint of a metal hand on one of the smiling group.

'Found you!' he breathed. 'I've found you, Jake Moss!'

Edward did not feel so elated halfway through the following morning as he bent over the rails of HMS Elmdon, retching into the North Sea, much to the amusement of her crew. Train travel had been out of the question; he could not get a permit. In any case, there wasn't a direct line that ran from London to Edinburgh.

'One hour to go,' he groaned, 'Then at least I can stand on dry land.'

At last, Edward tottered down the gangplank and stood swaying at Leith Docks. From here, it would be a three-mile walk to the offices of The Scotsman. Hopefully, by the time he reached his destination, the tidal waves rippling through his stomach would have subsided.

'So, you don't know where they were going when they left, but perhaps someone else will. Do you know where else they went to in Edinburgh?'

Edward left the newspaper offices and attempted to retrace the steps of the airship's crew. He couldn't glean any more information from the hotel where they had eaten and the various clothes shops they had visited. Obviously, everybody remembered them - nothing so exciting had happened in the city for a long time - but nobody had any idea where the airship was heading. Finally, Edward walked into Bruce Robertson's clockwork supply shop and explained that he was writing an article about airship travel.

'Och! I've known Oliver Moon for years!' said Bruce, 'Mechanical parts from this shop are why he can soar through the skies. Mind you, it was the new boy who was doing all the choosing this time.'

'Would that be Jake Moss?'

'Aye, well Jake was his first name, I dinnae ken his second name.'

'Do you know where they were going after they left Edinburgh?'

'They never said, but I imagine they were going where he normally goes.'

'Which is?'

'Why, Foula.'

'Foula!' Edward exclaimed in delight. 'What direction is it? How long would it take me to walk.'

'It's North. You could try walking, but you would get awful wet!' Bruce laughed. 'It's in the Shetland Isles, a long, three hundred and eighty-mile boat ride from here.

'A boat! Oh no!' groaned Edward, and his stomach quivered at the mere thought of it.

CHAPTER ELEVEN

'I'm sorry I haven't been very good company,' said Edward as he deposited his lunch over the side of the boat. The fisherman who had brought him to Foula laughed at the sight of this sea-sick sassenach, slapped him on the back and then pointed him toward the Laird's house. As pleased as Edward was to be on dry land, the black cloud on the horizon was the thought that to leave, he would have to cross the seas once more.

Edward's heart was beating fast as he knocked on the door to The Haa. Was this a den of murdering thieves? The man who answered the door looked very similar to the man in the newspaper photograph. Maybe he was the ringleader.

'Hello. My name is Edward Ramsey…'

'Ah! Come in, come in. It's too windy to be standing

with the door open. I'm the Laird, Alexander Moon; what can I do for you?' Edward had decided to keep to the same cover story he had used in Edinburgh, that he was researching airships to write an article, but he faltered.

'There's an Alexander Moon who is a poet. I don't suppose…'

'The very same.'

'I can't believe it. I studied your poems when I was at university.'

'And do you write?'

'Oh, just pieces for newspapers, but nothing worthwhile.' They sat at the table and talked about literature over a cup of tea for the next hour, then gradually, more and more people arrived and joined them until suddenly it dawned on Edward that all the people in the newspaper photograph were present. They were joking, laughing, and tucking into a plate of stew the young boy had cooked. Edward complimented the chef:

'This is delicious, I can't tell you how sick I felt earlier. Thank you for making me so welcome.' Then he felt a pang of guilt, 'Actually, I have to tell you the truth about why I am here.'

'I wondered when you would get around to that,' laughed Alexander. 'Nobody just happens to be passing Foula. You have to put in some effort to get here.' The others fell silent, as Edward told them the full story of how everyone he had met had tried to discourage him from investigating further and how he had been told that Joshua was a thief. After an initial clamour, with everyone trying to speak at once, it was Charlotte who asserted control.

'Did you speak to my father?'

'No, he wouldn't see me. I just spoke to Hastings.'

'That brute,' she retorted. Then she proceeded to tell

the tale from the point of view of herself and her friends.

'I must tell you that Hastings is scouring the country for you. I think he's probably still in England, but if he gets to Edinburgh, I imagine he will be able to pick up the trail. You caused quite a stir. What I can't understand is this: I can see why Hastings wants revenge on you, Jake, as you bashed him on the head, but why are Fotheringay and the army putting so much effort into finding you? Why did they bother painting your old room?'

'I can tell you that,' replied Jake. 'They know, from the drawings on my walls, that I was on to them. I didn't understand it then, but I do now. I've worked out that they plan to produce a weapon more deadly than anything that has ever gone before. They have harnessed the combined power of steam and clockwork to create a giant cannon that could send thousands of gas capsules three times as far as gunpowder could.'

'Gas capsules?' queried Oliver.

'Yes, they will break open on impact, releasing deadly gases; the kind that would burn you from the inside when you breathed, but because of the distances involved, there would be no danger to the people operating the cannon.'

'I've never heard anything so cowardly in my life!' Oliver exploded, banging his fist on the table, 'Where's the honour in that?'

'I have been studying the design, and I think I can detect a weakness, but it would require powerful magnets to disarm the cannon,' said Jake.

'Where d'yer get magnets from?' asked Billy.

'I was studying them in the Library before we left London. I know there is a major supplier in Bristol.'

'Then we should go there and do something about this,' declared Oliver 'Are you with me, crew?' Jake, Joshua and Billy roared, 'Yessss!'

'Might I make a suggestion,' said Charlotte, level-headed as always. 'We know Hastings is searching for us, probably visiting major cities you can reach by train. The last place we want him to arrive is here. What if we lead him away from Foula by flying low over Edinburgh and Glasgow and then visit all the major cities in the West as we travel down to Bristol? Then perhaps we could travel over the countryside at night for our return to London.'

'An excellent idea,' said Oliver, 'It's been a positive time here on Foula. I feel clear-headed and strong and my cracked ribs have healed. You've all spent your time well: Jake, I'm looking forward to seeing how you've improved the airship; Joshua, I'm sure the widow will be thanking you all winter, given the surprising amount of peat you have cut; Billy, life will improve no end, now we have an onboard cook, and Charlotte, I know you have been busy with a needle and thread. Bring all your sewing kit with you; there will be a stitch and a snip you can make to all our clothes. It's important that we cut a sartorial dash, and of course, you remain the chief pilot. Say your goodbyes to the island and its folk. We will leave tomorrow at first light. Now, Edward, are you one of us, or do you simply want a lift back to London, albeit taking a long, scenic route?'

'I would definitely like a ride back to London, and it's not just because I can't face another boat trip. I want to get to know you all better. I will give you my full support, but I think I will be more useful to you on land. While trying to track you down, I had an interesting conversation with a man called Paul Reuter in the telegraph offices. He has started a company providing business news to banks and now wants to broaden it to distribute other news using the telegraph service. He's looking for roving reporters and I have an interview for a job with him next week.'

'Capital! We are the eyes up in the sky, and you can be our ears on the ground! I'll drink to that!' Oliver strode over to where the bottle of whisky had perched on a shelf since he arrived, poured a good measure into his empty teacup and downed it in one. Charlotte's eyes rolled. The old Oliver was back and he would have a hangover tomorrow when it was time to back the airship out of its hiding place in the cliff.

Edward was up early the following day and he and Alexander nursed cups of tea while they talked about books.

'The thing is,' explained Edward, 'I'm not like you. I don't hear love calling in the wind and feel heartbreak in the crashing waves. I would like to write stories like Charles Dickens, Lewis Carroll, or H. G. Wells.'

'Then why don't you?'

'I've never had anything to write about.'

'You have now!'

Everyone enjoyed the flight over Edinburgh and Glasgow, including the onlookers. Charlotte steered the airship expertly along the Water of Leith and the River Clyde, and Joshua made the most of the fact that, as they were still in Scotland, he could don his tartan cloak again and climb down the ladder to wave regally to the cheering crowds.

They headed south and cruised over Manchester, following the railway tracks and travelling west towards Liverpool. They weren't planning to stop, but Charlotte spotted something alarming.

'Oh no!' she cried, pointing. Ahead of them was a railway station, a long structure with a flat roof and a parapet running the length of the building. 'Do you see him?'

'Who?' answered Jake,

'There! On the station roof. That young boy. He looks like he's trying to pluck up enough courage to jump to his death.' Charlotte pulled hard on the controls, so that the airship swung round and hovered above the station. She desperately hoped the boy wouldn't be distracted by their arrival and lose his balance, but he seemed totally focused on the tracks below. They were flying very low now, and Jake threw the rope ladder through the door.

'I'll go,' said Charlotte, 'Oliver, please can you take over the helm?'

'Aye, aye, Captain,' he replied with a salute and a smile. Charlotte climbed gingerly down the ladder and approached the boy. He was still standing at the roof's edge and didn't seem to realise she was there.

'Hello, don't be alarmed. I won't come any closer. I want to help.'

'Nowt you can do. My life won't be worth living when I get home, so I may as well end it now. Anyway, there will be fewer mouths to feed, so they'll be glad of it!'

'No, you mustn't do that. What can be so terrible that you would think about doing that? Please sit down; you're making me nervous standing there.' The boy turned and sat on the parapet wall.

'Me mam gave me some money to buy bread, but I bumped into the Scuttlers, and they took it off me.'

'Scuttlers? What are they?'

'Aven't you heard of the Scuttlers? They're the biggest street-fighting gang around here.'

'I'm not from around here; I came in that,' replied Charlotte, pointing to the airship.'

'Blimey! How did I not notice that?'

'Do you want to come and look? We can give you a loaf of bread. My name's Charlotte.'

'Not half!' said the boy, jumping up. 'I'm Micky.'

Thirty minutes later, having walked an awe-struck Micky home bearing a loaf of bread and a joint of ham so large that his mother's eyes nearly popped out, Oliver, Joshua, Jake and Edward returned to Liverpool Road Station, while Charlotte, back at the helm, kept the airship hovering above it. They were almost there, when out of the station entrance, filed a group of around twenty youths. Oliver stiffened. They were all dressed alike with flat caps, checked silk scarves knotted around their necks and wide, bell-bottomed trousers.

'Keep your wits about you,' Oliver said quietly. He knew that wearing a distinctive 'uniform' was the tell-tale sign of a gang member. The young men fanned out and surrounded the crew. Instinctively, Oliver and Joshua halted whilst Jake and Edward moved behind them and turned to face the threat.

'What are they doing?' whispered Jake, 'Some of them are undoing their belts!'

'Weapons,' was the reply from Oliver. The belts all had over-large buckles. Some gang members wrapped their belts around their fists, creating lethal knuckle-dusters; others swung them in menacing arcs. The circle of hostility gradually closed in.

'It seems violence is inevitable,' said Oliver calmly, holding his cane in both hands. Only Jake knew that this innocent-looking walking stick contained a sharp sword. Then, suddenly, several of the gang rushed at them. Everything happened very quickly. One of them swung his belt at Oliver's head, but not before Oliver had drawn his sword and sliced clean through it. The buckle clattered at Oliver's feet, and he quickly picked it up and stuffed it in his pocket. Another youth, with a belt around his fist, swung a punch at Edward, but Edward sidestepped him and delivered three swift jabs to his assailant's jaw, followed by a punch to the stomach. As his opponent crumpled to the ground, Edward grabbed hold of the belt and pulled it free. Another belt came swinging through the air, this time aimed at Jake, who raised his arm to ward it off. Fortunately for him, it was his left arm. The belt wrapped itself around his wrist, and the sharpened buckle clanged against his metal hand. He yanked hard, and the gang member, who had expected to have inflicted considerable damage on Jake, stumbled and found himself in the arms of Joshua, who lifted him as easily as he would lift a hay bale and then flung him at another approaching youth.

The circle widened again, and everyone eyed each other warily. Some youths now held knives, but they knew they were only useful at close quarters, and Oliver's sword stick proved an effective deterrent. It was stalemate until, to the gang's surprise, a rope ladder appeared out of thin air. Oliver put a steadying foot on the bottom rung.

'After you, gents,' he said. Edward went first, followed by Jake. Oliver insisted Joshua climb onto it next whilst he continued to swish his sword about him. The gang stood frozen to the spot; open-mouthed in amazement. The moment Oliver placed both of his feet on the bottom rung of the ladder, Charlotte swung hard on a lever, and the airship rose in the air, well out of the gang's reach.

'I think we have just been introduced to Manchester's Scuttlers,' said Edward once they were aboard.

'That's a fearsome left jab you have there,' remarked Oliver. 'I didn't expect it from you. I thought you were just a scribbler!

'I represented Oxford University at boxing,' replied Edward, 'Although the only people I fought against were Cambridge University students.'

'Could you give me a few tips?' asked Jake.

'Be glad to,' replied Edward.

'I'm sorry I couldn't rescue you earlier,' said Charlotte, 'There was a bit of a headwind and I was nervous about getting it wrong.'

'Nonsense!' replied Oliver, tossing the buckle he had acquired onto the deck. 'You did very well. Any earlier, and you would have spoiled the fun.'

'Actually,' said Edward, noticing the belt still wrapped around Jake's metal hand, 'Would you mind if I kept the belts and buckles as souvenirs?'

'Why? Are yer trousers falling down?' laughed Billy.

'No, before I left Foula, I told Alexander I didn't know what to write about, but now I do. When I get to London, I will see if I can afford to get someone to print serialised stories about your exploits. The belts and buckles would make interesting illustrations to add colour to the tale.'

'I'll happily invest in your enterprise,' said Oliver.

'No,' replied Edward firmly, 'I think there would be more credibility if it was truly independent. You just need to continue having adventures. And if you don't - I'll have to make them up!'

CHAPTER TWELVE

'Have I seen an airship?'

'Yes.'

'What, here in Liverpool?'

'Well, have you?'

'You mean a big airship with a lightning bolt on the side?'

'Yes, yes!'

'Gizza penny, an I'll tell you where I saw it.'

'You better not be lying.'

'I'm not, honest to God. Gizza penny.' Hastings handed over the coin.

'Well! Where did you see it?'

'Just there.' The boy pointed over Hastings' shoulder at an airship gliding past, following the course of the

Mersey.

'Why you…' but the boy was gone.

After Liverpool, Charlotte steered the airship south to Birmingham, and after a low pass over the city to wave at the crowds, she then turned the nose southwest.

'You seem to fly effortlessly,' said Jake, full of admiration.

'I'm trying hard not to be too complacent, but I hardly have to think about it at all now. It helps to have you doing the navigation. Especially as Oliver is asleep because he flew through the night.'

'It's good that Oliver remained sober because he showed me how to navigate using a map and compass. I love all these charts and measurements.'

'I must admit, I was a little concerned when Oliver toasted the success of our venture back in Scotland that he would get a taste for alcohol again.'

'Joshua is asleep too because he stayed up late. Did you know that he is adept at navigating by the stars, a skill he learned as a sailor on the west coast of Africa?'

'Look, I can see the glint of the ocean ahead.'

'Good, follow the coastline. You will be flying down through Gloucestershire to the River Avon, where you can swing the airship to the east heading towards the morning sun and follow the river to the city of Bristol.'

'Fine, I won't need you for a while then. You can go back to your training.'

Jake and Edward had spent many hours together, shadowboxing and improving Jake's defending tactics. Edward had taken the precaution of wrapping Jake's left hand in fabric. He certainly didn't want to risk an accidental blow from a metal fist!

'You're looking very promising,' said Edward, 'Now you need to work on your strength and stamina. Just don't panic in a fight, keep a cool head and wait for an opportunity, knowing that you have a lethal weapon attached to your left hand.'

Billy was pleased that he did not have to spend so much time winding the clockwork engine, thanks to Jake's improvements, and he spent much of his day preparing food. He insisted that they had to stop and lower a cauldron to the ground once a day. He would then climb down the ladder to cook a stew on an open fire. He was also experimenting with different recipes for biscuits and buns cooked in a cast-iron pot on the fire. He luxuriated in the knowledge that he was the most popular person on the airship when he climbed back up and dished out the food.

Jake didn't know exactly where the magnet supplier was, but he had an excellent memory and remembered that it was somewhere in the Fishponds district. The plan was that they would journey down to the centre of Bristol, following the river, and then swing back around to the North-East and find Fishponds.

'Oh look!' said Charlotte. 'They are building a bridge.' On each side of the river were high cliffs, and a stone tower rose from either side of the gorge.

'Slow down,' said Jake, who loved anything to do with engineering, 'This is interesting.'

A rowing boat was making its way across the river below them. A steel chain, tied to a rope, was being hauled across the river in the opposite direction by a team of men. Then, disaster! The chain appeared to snag; the workers continued to pull, but the rope snapped and the chain swung down, heading back across the gorge. The chain crashed into the rowing boat, slicing a section off the stern. The boat started to sink. Fortunately, the men weren't hurt, but they stayed in the boat as the cold waters of the River Avon swirled around them.

'I don't think they can swim!' cried Charlotte in alarm, 'Or else why are they still sitting there?'

'Take us down, Charlotte,' yelled Joshua. 'I can swim!'

Charlotte pulled on levers and flipped the propellers, and the airship began to descend. Joshua pulled off his boots and stood in the open doorway, but they were going too slowly! The boat had disappeared now, and the men were flailing about in the water, then one man sank out of sight. Without a moment's thought, Joshua launched himself from the airship and plummeted some hundred and fifty-feet into the river. He entered the water like a bullet and, opening his eyes as he shot deeper and deeper, he saw one of the rowers sinking to the bottom of the river. As Joshua made contact with the river bed he kicked his way upwards, grabbing the drowning man's collar as he rose to the surface. The other rower was clinging onto a piece of wreckage from the boat as it swept downstream towards the sea.

'Hold on!' shouted Joshua, 'We will come back for you!' He looked up and saw that the rope ladder from the airship was nearly within reach. He struck out for it, dragging the dead weight of the rower with him and managed to grab onto it. He climbed slowly up the ladder, with one arm clutching the rower. From the airship, Oliver and Jake hauled on the ladder until pretty soon Joshua was bent over, panting from his efforts, and the rower was lying lifeless on the deck.

'Is he alright or 'as 'e snuffed it?' asked Billy.

'Somewhere in-between,' Joshua replied, then he

dropped to his knees next to the rower and started to knead the man's stomach and chest, 'I saw this work when I was a sailor.' After a few moments, the man spluttered, coughed up a bellyful of river water and lay on his back, dazed and exhausted. Finally, he uttered the words:

'Am I in heaven? I thought it would be bigger.'

Meanwhile, Charlotte did not need to be told to follow the other rower. Even before Joshua had reached the gondola, she had started to wheel the airship about. Billy gave the clockwork mechanism a few extra winds - now was not the time for the engines to falter. Charlotte was surprised by how far the man had travelled, but eventually, she caught him up, positioning the airship above him, and this time Jake went down the ladder. The stranded man required considerable coaxing because he was reluctant to let go of the piece of the boat that he was holding onto.

'You have to, man,' yelled Jake, reaching out with his right hand. 'Or else you will end up lost at sea!' The man seized the outstretched hand. Jake's metal hand was clasped firmly around the ladder, so Jake knew he had no risk of falling, and he was able to guide the man to safety.

When the airship returned to the bridge and the two rowers climbed down to the ground, the rest of the workforce was assembled and cheering. They gestured for the crew to join them, so Charlotte tethered the airship to one of the chains attached to the bridge. When they had all climbed down, they found themselves in the middle of an impromptu party. From somewhere, crates of beer appeared, and an engineer, his face smeared with grease, cheerily handed the bottles around. Jake was too polite to refuse and pretended to drink, knowing he could secretly pass his bottle on to Oliver.

'Oh no!' thought Charlotte, as she saw how much Oliver was relishing the taste of the beer. Some of the workers were Irish, they produced their fiddles and the cliffs echoed to the sound of Irish jigs. Suddenly, one of them seized Charlotte, and to her surprise, he whisked her away to join the dancing. Her first instinct was to resist - the kind of dancing she was used to being altogether more sedate. However, like Jake, she felt that refusing such generous hospitality would be impolite so she began to dance. Then, as she whirled around, she realised she was rather enjoying it. After several dances, she joined Jake, who was standing to one side, appreciating the spectacle. Another man approached.

'Oh! No more dancing,' protested Charlotte, 'I'm exhausted.'

'Forgive me; I merely wanted to thank you for saving the two men. My name is Isaiah Tompkins. I'm the foreman.'

'Anyone would have done it,' replied Charlotte.

'Not everyone has an airship,' said Isaiah with a smile.

'Does this bridge have a name?' asked Jake.

'Yes, a very descriptive one. It's the Clifton Suspension Bridge.'

'I thought it was!' replied Jake excitedly, 'I've read about it. Isambard Kingdom Brunel designed it, didn't he? When he was only twenty-four - just a few years older than me!'

'True.'

'I love engineering. Perhaps you can help me. I don't suppose you know of a magnet manufacturer in Fishponds.

'I certainly do. It's very close to George Adlam & Sons, the iron and brass foundry, managed by my father-in-law.'

'Oh, heaven!' replied Jake, 'Magnets, a foundry, bridge-building! This is my kind of place!'

'I'll write you a letter of introduction,' said Isaiah, 'I'm sure they could make anything you want at a generous discount.'

'Tell me,' said Charlotte, 'Am I right in thinking that the unfortunate rowers were taking the rope over to the other side of the river so you could pull the chain across?'

'That's correct, only now we don't have a boat.'

'Why don't we help? We could easily take your cable across by fixing it to the airship,' said Charlotte excitedly.

'Oh, yes! I would be honoured to contribute to the project,' added Jake.

'It doesn't look as though the rest of your men are fit for work,' Charlotte smiled, gesturing to the party in full progress. Then she noticed Oliver clasping a beer bottle and kicking his legs up in time to an Irish Jig and Billy asleep on the ground with several empty bottles beside him. 'It doesn't look like a couple of our air crew are ready for action either!' Edward was still sober, but he was interviewing people and writing in a notebook, and Joshua was deep in conversation with the only black worker there. They were slapping each other on the back and roaring with laughter. 'The job only needs two of us, anyway,' said Charlotte cheerily.

That afternoon Jake and Oliver spent their time shopping but sought out very different items. Oliver walked from Clifton into the centre of town. He said the walk would clear his head. Charlotte hoped he wouldn't drop into one of the many pubs en route, which would undo all the benefits of the walk. The others all climbed back into the airship, although Billy got there by being hoisted onto Joshua's shoulders because he was quite intoxicated. Jake climbed out at Fishponds and went to buy magnets.

There was a time in his previous life as a cleaner when the doorman wouldn't have let Jake over the threshold of such an establishment. Now, with his finely-tailored clothes, a purse containing Oliver's money in his pocket and a pair of leather gloves concealing his metal hand, he entered full of confidence. He knew exactly what he wanted, and the sales manager appreciated Jake's scientific knowledge and inquisitive nature. Meanwhile, Charlotte slowly circled above, keeping well away from the chimneys of the nearby foundry. One spark from there could ignite the airship, ending her new career - and her life.

Once he had bought the magnets, Jake visited the company recommended by the bridge engineer to buy a piece of sheet metal.

'I'm impressed by the set-up here at George Adlam & Sons. I would like to use you for future projects. I am a design engineer.'

'Certainly, Sir. Come to the office, and we will set up credit arrangements.

As for the pot of paint and paintbrush you wanted, please accept these, courtesy of the company.' The sales manager could never have guessed just how proud Jake felt to describe himself as a design engineer!

When he climbed on board the airship, Jake noticed that Joshua had taken over clockwork winding duties from Billy. The boy was still asleep! Charlotte set the airship on course for Clifton whilst Jake immediately set to work with the brush and paint.

'What are you painting, Jake?' called Charlotte. Jake held up the piece of metal, and Charlotte gasped, letting go of the controls and clapping a hand to her mouth. The airship shuddered, almost in sympathy, and started to veer off course. Charlotte had to quickly turn and wrestle with the controls to get the airship to fly in the right direction. Jake had painted a very accurate representation of the logotype for her father's company, Fotheringay's Steam Works, on the metal plate.

'Why?' she stuttered. 'Why are you painting that?' Jake's face fell.

'I'm sorry, Charlotte, I'm an idiot! I should have mentioned it before I started. I've got so used to thinking of us as a team that I forgot about your past life. It's part of my plan to disable the Tiberius weapon.'

'There is no need to apologise, Jake. It was just a bit of a shock. I'm trying to blot out that part of my life. I realise now that I never truly knew my father. I clearly only saw one side of him; I would never have guessed that he could be involved in making such a despicable instrument of war.'

'It must be difficult for you. I was only fifteen when my parents were killed, so I never got to know them as an adult. In fact, even when I was a child, I didn't see that much of them because they were so busy working to make ends meet.'

'Working to make my father rich!' said Charlotte bitterly. She was troubled, and despite putting on a confident front for Jake, she was full of self-doubt. What kind of daughter would turn against her parents in the way that she had? Admittedly, they hadn't had much to do with her upbringing - that was the responsibility of her Nannie. Until that dreadful day in the factory when he would not let her join the Air-Fleet, her father had never refused her anything. Was she just an ungrateful wretch who deserved punishment?

The airship was once again moored to the bridge at Clifton. Oliver climbed the ladder; he was carrying a bag so large that there was a real risk of it being caught by the wind and blown away. He struggled through the gondola door, took a moment to catch his breath, and then announced:

'Hats!'

'Wot?' asked Billy, by now awake but nursing a headache.

'Hats! I decided we need more hats.' Oliver emptied the bag onto the floor and revealed dozens of hats; mostly top hats and bowler hats. 'I went into a shop to buy a new hat and discovered they were selling up and leaving. The gangs are extorting money from them with the threat of extreme violence, and they have had enough! As elsewhere, the police are overwhelmed and are concentrating their efforts on protecting the richer areas of the city, while the army has retreated. So this particular hatter thought it was time for early retirement. I bought up his stock. Some of them require finishing off - a little embellishment. Hats for everyone.' Oliver selected a top hat and placed it on Charlotte's head. She giggled and adjusted the hat to a jauntier angle. Oliver noted that it was the first time he had seen Charlotte laugh freely since he had known her.

'Embellishment! I've got just the thing!' cried Jake, and he reached under his seat and pulled out a sack. 'Look!' He delved into it and produced a handful of cogs. 'There are loads of them. I got them from the foundry in Fishponds. Some are imperfect; others were over-ordered. They were going to melt them down, but I persuaded the foreman to give them to me.' He looked towards Charlotte.

'Hmm, if only we knew someone who could sew.' Charlotte giggled again; Oliver applauded and threw his hat across the gondola, to be joined by dozens more thrown by the rest of the crew.

CHAPTER THIRTEEN

It was early morning when the airship ghosted into London on a grey foggy day. She had flown through the night, above the clouds, to shake off anyone following, and the murky weather was ideal for a secret arrival. Billy was the first to climb down the ladder at Blackwall. After a quick scout around, he waved his top hat to signal that nothing looked amiss. The planks of wood hiding the entrance to the tunnel did not appear to have been disturbed. Billy began hauling them to one side, and Joshua and Edward joined in. If Charlotte had thought that guiding the airship into the crevice in Foula was difficult, this was ten times trickier because Oliver insisted that she reverse the airship into place.

'That's my girl! I knew you could do it!' Charlotte gave

a satisfied smile. Then Oliver roared, 'Are we ready, crew? Now is the time to turn and face them. Now is the time to fight!'

By the time they arrived at the entrance to The Rookery, it was mid-morning. They had parted company with Edward, who had a job interview with Reuters and a plan to visit publishing houses to see if they would be interested in his stories. He arranged to meet the crew at the Rat and Whippet that evening.

'Well, I never!' remarked Jake. 'The gates are gone.'

'And so are the soldiers,' added Oliver. They had barely gone ten steps before a familiar sight greeted them - a line of young men, each wearing a bowler hat with a rook's feather tucked into the band, was blocking the street .

'Good morning, people,' said one, 'I have to inform you that this is a toll road and to progress any further you will have to pay the sum of one shilling.' Charlotte placed a steadying hand on Oliver's sleeve. She knew what his likely reaction would be.

'We don't want any trouble,' she whispered. 'We don't want anyone to notice us, we're on a mission.' She felt Oliver stiffen, but then he relaxed.

'Allow me to compensate you for the sterling work you chaps are doing,' he said, removing his top hat, bowing and handing over five shillings. 'Your efforts have not gone unnoticed,' he added, looking each gang member in the eye, an act that seemed to make them feel uncomfortable. 'Good day.'

Jake chuckled, 'We don't want to be noticed! Look at us, dressed up to the nines, wearing hats and clothes decorated with cogs. We include a giant of a black man in a tartan cape, a lady wearing clothes in a style that no woman has worn before, not to mention the goggles we have around our necks or on our hats.'

'There is such a thing,' replied Oliver with a laugh, 'As hiding in plain sight, and that is precisely what we are doing. No one will expect us to have returned here. Hopefully, Hastings will still be following the trail we laid down the West Coast of England. Come on, let's go and see how Carrington is recovering.'

The Cabinet meeting was in session and its members were bickering.

'Order! Order!' shouted Field Marshal Bellings, 'I insist that we have unity. We must adapt to the circumstances. We are all army men, and I will always put the needs of the army first, but we have to face facts. Without cooperation from the Navy, we cannot transport our troops around the perimeter of this country. The train network is inadequate. Therefore we have to admit at least three Jack Tars to this cabinet. I propose the Admiral of the Fleet and a couple of regular Admirals.'

'I hope you will not co-opt any of those jumped-up airborne types.'

'Good God, no, of course not! Now, there is another good reason for this move. I ask you this. Throughout history, whenever the population has been disgruntled, divided or downright rebellious, what has united them?'

'Why, going to war, of course.'

'Exactly. And since the horse flu hit our shores, the population has never been so troublesome, what with food shortages, unemployment and the rising threat of street gangs.'

'War, eh! So who do you suppose we fight?

'Oh! Anyone we can beat. It hardly matters who. But, we will need the Navy on board, if you'll pardon the pun, which brings me to the forthcoming trial of Fotheringay's secret weapon.'

'I wonder why the curtains are closed?' pondered Oliver as he knocked on Cissie Newton's door. 'Maybe old Carrington is having a snooze.' The door was opened by Cissie. She looked worn out, her face had lost any colour, and there were dark shadows below her eyes. She managed a weak smile.

'Come in. How did you know?'

'How did we know what?' asked Oliver.

'Oh, I thought that's why you'd come. The doctor predicts that my brother has only hours to live. Miss Fotheringay, he was asking after you. Would you like to see him?' Charlotte's eyes welled up and her bottom lip trembled. It was all she could do to nod her agreement.

'I'll come with you,' said Oliver, taking her arm. Cissie showed them into the bedroom, where Carrington lay motionless on the bed.

'Oh, Carrington!' cried Charlotte. He turned his head and smiled.

'Miss Fotheringay,' he gasped, 'And Group Captain Moon, so glad you could both come. I know I haven't got long left on this earth.'

'I don't know what to say. I am so sorry my family is responsible for this,' said Charlotte.

'It's not your fault.' Carrington was finding it difficult to talk; his voice was just a whisper, 'In many ways, I have brought it upon myself. I knew that certain aspects of your father's business practices were underhand, but I turned a blind eye. Perhaps this is divine retribution.'

'Oh, it's not fair,' cried Charlotte.

'You have my word,' said Oliver, 'A line has been drawn. My crew and I are on one side of it, and Fotheringay and his cronies are on the other.'

'I'm tired,' whispered the old man, 'Leave me now. Please get Cissie.' Oliver and Charlotte joined the others who were waiting in the kitchen. A few minutes later, they heard sobs from Cissie and knew Carrington was dead.

Charlotte decided to stay and try to comfort Cissie. She felt numb. Oliver, on the other hand, was full of pent-up anger. He needed to get out of the house, or else he feared he would lose control and smash something. He stumbled out into the daylight, Joshua and Billy following him. They had never met Carrington before and didn't feel comfortable invading Cissie's privacy.

'Stay here; we'll come back and get you in a while,' said Jake to Charlotte. 'We've arranged to meet Edward in the pub later, but I have a strong feeling that Oliver is heading there now. We had better keep an eye on him.'

Jake ran after the others. He saw Joshua's tartan cloak disappearing down a passageway and sprinted to catch up. He was wrong about Oliver heading for the Rat. At the end of the alley was a dingy-looking pub called 'The Dead-End Tavern'. As Oliver slipped through the scratched and decrepit front door, he paid no heed to the rest of the crew.

'Anyone want a drink?' asked Jake. Billy shook his head, remembering his last encounter with alcohol in Bristol.

'Too early in the day for me,' said Joshua 'I like a drink after a hard day's work but I haven't done anything yet.'

'Let's just wait for him outside then,' said Jake.

They sat in the shadows on a wall opposite the pub, keeping an eye on the door, and each sank into their own thoughts. The elation they had all felt as they glided through the mist into London that morning had evaporated.

Joshua had enjoyed the cheering and clapping from the crowds on the journey from Scotland, but now that was over his thoughts turned to his life before slave traders captured him. He knew it was a world he could not return to - he had seen too much - but Joshua's heart grew heavy at the thought of other Africans destined for a life of slavery, and he felt powerless to do anything about it.

Billy felt ashamed. He had set himself a goal to provide good, healthy meals for the crew and had failed by getting drunk in Bristol. The others had been forced to survive on cold pork and bread. Now that he was in an unfamiliar part of London, he didn't know his role. He had no desire to return to the East End, but how could he contribute here?

It was different for Jake. These streets and alleyways were familiar to him and threw into sharp contrast just how much he had changed. Not only did he look different in his fancy clothes, but he had also found the means to put some of the plans bursting out of his head into action. He had manufactured his metal hand and already had ideas to improve it. He had re-designed the clockwork mechanism that powered the airship and knew he could do so much more. However, his focus now had to be to disarm Fotheringay's Tiberius weapon. He had detected a fault in the cannon's engineering but couldn't see a way to use that knowledge. He knew they needed to work as a team, but one member, their mentor and inspiration, was inside the Dead-End Tavern, drowning his sorrows.

Oliver

I'm looking around this pub, and it's half empty, like my glass. God, it's a dreary place. I don't know why I came here. To be honest, it was the nearest and I needed a drink. Not wanted, needed! It's hard remembering a time when I didn't drink. We had some fine old drunken times when I was at University. I was fearless then and I still am; I remember scaling the clock tower and tying a pair of ladies' bloomers to it. I wonder where I got those from? I hope, for the young owner's sake that it wasn't a breezy walk home! I don't remember anything about lectures and studying at University; everything I know comes from being out there, living life. Did I get a degree? Don't know. I suppose I must have, but I didn't need it because I took up a commission in the army. Obviously, people would say that I became an officer not on my own merit but because of my father's connections, and I hate to admit it, but they would be right. My father was rich and had his finger in a lot of pies. It was the country estate in Yorkshire that I was most familiar with. That's where my brother and I would return to in the holidays from boarding school, but I know he had shares in factories and mills in Manchester and Leeds. I try and block out thoughts about the conditions the kids working there had to endure. And the best way to do that - "Barman! Another drink here!" Add a few years to the ages of those factory kids and you've got some of the infantrymen in the regiments I served with. More faces to block out. Some died with honour, fighting bravely for their Queen. Others went to their maker trembling with fear, being ordered to march towards certain death. One thing I could always do was fight. "Barman! Another drink, damn you!" It was as if time stood still in a battle, and I could stride forward and smite the enemy at will. My problems arrived once the battle was over. Then I would drink until the shaking stopped. One dreadful day I received a message from an orderly, but before I opened it, I poured myself a drink, then another and afterwards slipped into sleep. When I eventually awoke and found the letter on my lap, I read to my horror that it was a request for reinforcements to be sent to the front. When my men got there it was too late, and the beleaguered soldiers were all dead. My superiors kept the reason for the delay quiet, but I was moved to another regiment, and then another, and another. Finally, I was transferred to the Air-Fleet, something the High Command thought of as a demotion. The Air-Fleet had no tradition, no history, no status, but it was the saving of me. It didn't rescue my military career though, I had more and more run-ins with my superior officers, most of whom were jackasses, but the sensation of flying allowed me to transcend my insular life and rise to a new plane of existence. I felt it then and I still feel it today. "Barman, drinks all round; I'll sing you a sad Scottish song:

"Ye banks and braes o' bonnie Doon,
How can ye bloom sae fresh and fair?
How can ye chant, ye little birds,
And I sae weary, fu' o' care!"

'Penny for them?' asked the landlord. Oliver had fallen silent and was staring into his glass. He ignored the barman's question. His thoughts were too dark to be shared, even in a grimy, miserable pub like this. He had always been good at two things, drinking and fighting, but now the beer didn't always make him happy.

'Another drink?' asked the landlord.

'Yes, but not here,' Oliver growled, as he slid off his bar stool and staggered out of the pub.

Shielding his eyes against the bright sunlight, Oliver set off for The Rat and Whippet, followed, at a distance, by his guardians, Jake, Joshua and Billy.

'Take note of the route,' said Jake, 'In case one of you has to come back for Charlotte later.' Joshua nodded, pulled out a knife and scratched three lines into the wall they were passing. He kept this up through the maze of streets until once more they were sitting on a wall outside a pub. This time it was the Rat.

Oliver's mood lifted the moment he walked into the pub. He greeted the barman and bought him and the other four people in the pub a drink. He then proceeded to entertain the customers with tales of various inns and taverns he had frequented in his travels throughout Europe. They were an eager audience; the drinks kept coming as long as they listened and laughed. Oliver had just finished telling them about a particularly entertaining evening in Amsterdam's red light district when he remembered Madame Boo-Boo's, and Trixie. Oliver's guardian angels transferred themselves to a different wall. They had no more desire to enter a brothel than to frequent a public house.

Oliver was by now full of bonhomie, but his good humour was about to change rapidly.

'If you've come for Trixie, she's not available.'

'Oh, I can wait.'

'No, you're not understanding me; she's not available; she's reserved.'

'What do you mean, reserved?

'I mean just that. An officer is paying us a healthy retainer, so she is exclusive to him. I ain't going to risk that, no matter how good a customer you've been in the past. And before you ask, Sadie ain't available either. She had a bit of a bad time with a client, and she's locked her door. She won't let anyone in her room.'

'What do you mean, a bad time?'

'Don't you worry about that; it's all been taken care of. The Black Feathers are involved now. They take a cut of the business and don't take too kindly to anyone who will harm their profits. From what I hear, the eels at the bottom of the Thames are feeding on that particular gentleman now.'

'Sadie will see me,' replied Oliver confidently, as he bounded up the stairs. After five minutes of banging on the door, calling to her, the Madam had had enough.

'I told you, she ain't seeing anyone. Have a care. There's other gals workin' now, you know. Come and have a glass of whisky.'

Thirty minutes later, after polishing off half a bottle of whisky, Oliver was gently propelled out of the establishment. His morose singing was proving bad for business.

'I think I had better follow him into the Rat,' said Jake to Billy and Joshua. 'It's lunchtime. I'm happy to have a glass of milk now. There's a pie shop around the corner. Get yourselves something to eat and bring one for Oliver and me too. We have to look after him. He's his own worst enemy.'

CHAPTER FOURTEEN

Billy pounded on Cissie's door until Charlotte opened it.

'Jake said to ask yer if yer could come. We're supposed to be meetin' Edward soon. Jake's wiv Oliver now, but 'e's proper, proper drunk. 'E keeps tryin' to 'ave a barney wiv people. 'E's right narked abaht somethin' wot 'appened to a twist called Sadie.'

'Sadie at Madam Boo-Boo's? Why is she a twist?'

'You know her?' exclaimed Billy, surprised that Charlotte should be familiar with such an establishment. 'Twist and twirl - girl!'

'Ah! She gave me a dress to wear when we were trying to escape,' explained Charlotte. 'I'll tell Cissie I'm going out. I'm staying here tonight.'

Outside the Rat and Whippet, Jake gave Charlotte some more details whilst Joshua went inside the pub to keep an eye on Oliver.

'I think Oliver is genuinely worried about Sadie, but she won't see him. You know Oliver; he's used to getting his own way, so he's alternately angry and sad,' said Jake. Charlotte nodded thoughtfully:

'I'm worried about Sadie too. I'm going to see if she will speak to me.'

Edward arrived at the pub in time to help Jake lay the sleeping Oliver on a bench. 'We had better look after his purse, or the pickpockets will have it,' said Jake. 'He won't mind treating you to a glass of port and me to a glass of milk. He's been buying drinks for complete strangers all day. I'll give a few coins to Billy; he said he needs to buy onions, potatoes and mutton. I'm looking forward to his next stew.'

Once Jake had returned with the drinks, Edward recounted the events of his day.

'A little disappointing, really. All is not lost, but it's not won either. I visited five or six printers, trying to find someone to produce and distribute my stories. The problem is, because I am not an established author, they want me to pay for the costs in advance, more money than I have available!'

'What about the interview with the man at Reuters?'

'Unfortunately, he was none too impressed with the work that I had done for The Times. Mr Reuter explained that he was looking for a more investigative approach than he had seen in the work I have done so far. He understood that I was at the beck and call of my editor and had only been allowed to cover stories that he sanctioned, but he said I must prove myself. I have a week to find a story worthy of his organisation. And to top it all, a letter arrived from my wife, Arabella. The servant looking after our house while she is with her parents has informed her that I haven't been staying at home lately, and Arabella is asking if I can take some leave from The Times. I haven't told her that they have sacked me. It's all rather depressing, really!'

Old Nick from the Foundry was sitting nearby and had been listening to the conversation.

'I couldn't help overhearing that you was looking for a printer,' he said, leaning across from his bar stool.

'That's right, Sir,' replied Edward.

'I don't suppose you tried Bloxham's?'

'No, I've never heard of them.'

'Well, you wouldn't have. They ain't very big on account of Jed Bloxham spending more time reading books than he does printing 'em. I have to regularly do repairs on his printing press. It's getting on a bit, just like Jed and me,' Old Nick laughed. 'He's in Cold Harbour Lane, not far from here. Tell him Old Nick sent you. Mind you, if he don't like what you've written, he'll show you the door!'

Charlotte climbed Madam Boo-Boo's' stairs, leaving Joshua standing tall and threatening in the hallway. They were a curious couple, a girl dressed in a hybrid style, masculine but with feminine touches, and her enormous black bodyguard.

'Sadie, Sadie, can I come in? It's Charlotte. Do you remember me? You gave me a dress.'

'Go away!'

'I can't, Sadie. I'm worried about you. Please let me in. I don't like it out here.'

At last, Sadie relented and opened her door, locking it again behind Charlotte.

'Oh, Sadie! What happened? Your face!' Charlotte rushed over to comfort Sadie, who had let fall her shawl to reveal a swollen and bruised cheek and a split lip.

'It was this customer; he's been coming here regular and he's always liked to knock me about a bit, and paid extra for it, but this time he took it too far. I'm bruised all over. I can hardly walk.'

'The monster! How could he!'

'It happens. Some blokes like to be a bit rough. Usually, it's them as have a hard time from their bosses, or else it's the men who have married into brass and have to toe the line. It makes 'em feel important, like. Eh, love, I'm not 'specially angry with 'im; I'm just jiggered. Tired of the whole business. Tryin' to earn a few bob has always been hard graft, but it's even harder now that the gangs have moved in. And we've got to do 'em favours which don't earn me owt 'cos they don't pay up. I'm not kiddin', I'm reet tired of it all. But what else can I do?' She laid her head in Charlotte's lap and, while Charlotte stroked her hair, the bruised and battered young girl began to weep.

'It's not really my place to say,' said Charlotte, 'But why don't you come with us? I'm sure Oliver won't mind. I'll ask him.'

'He come round 'ere before. He sounded drunk!'

'I fear he's even drunker now. But I'm sure he only wanted to help you.'

'Well, I wasn't in the mood for company, any kind of company, but I'm glad you're here now.'

'What do you think? Why not join us?'

'Well, the Black Feathers would be flamin' mad for a start.'

'That wouldn't bother Oliver. You should have seen his face when we made him pay a toll to the gang without kicking up a fuss! He was furious!'

'Anyway, what would I do? I wouldn't be giving any favours away. I'm done with all that.'

'Of course not! You would get to see places. I haven't told you the best part, Oliver has an airship. We've been all over the country.'

'Well, blow me! But if you can fly all over the country, what are you doing back 'ere in The Rookery?'

'It's a long story, we're trying to stop my father from testing a new weapon - a steam-powered cannon - but we don't know when or where it will happen, and now we are busy trying to look after Oliver, who's too drunk to care.'

'As it happens, I can do something to help after all. Trixie has got herself a Major, and he told her something about testing a cannon, and she told me, but I wasn't really listening. I can find out, though.'

'That would be marvellous. And will you come with us?'

'If I can find out what you want to know, I will. Then I will feel like I've made a contribution. Come back tomorrer.'

Joshua escorted Charlotte back to Cissie's house and then returned to help persuade Oliver to leave the pub. He tried coaxing him, but when that didn't work, he simply scooped him up and carried him outside, setting him down unsteadily on his feet. While Jake led Oliver, Joshua, Billy and Edward out of The Rookery. Oliver began to talk - if the drunken stream of consciousness could be called talking!

'We don't know where to go,' said Jake, 'Shall we find

a hotel for the night?'

'No, no, no,' insisted Oliver, 'I've got a pal. We can stay at his house. He's away in the country. It's in Baker Street.'

'I know where that is; I've delivered candles there, helping Maggie,' said Jake, relieved that he wouldn't have to persuade a hotel to accept such a drunken guest.

'I had better go home,' said Edward, 'I'm afraid there would be a terrible hoo-ha if I were to invite you back and word would doubtless get back to my wife. What number in Baker Street is it? I'll come and see you tomorrow.'

'Two two', Oliver sang back to him.

'I'll see you in the morning at number twenty-two,' replied Edward, 'Good night, gentlemen.'

Joshua supported Oliver all the way to Baker Street because, left to his own devices, Oliver would have staggered all over the road. Eventually, they arrived at number twenty-two.

'Is this it? It's all in darkness,' said Jake.

'Never been here before. My pal's gone to the country,' slurred Oliver, 'We have to go round the back. The key should be under a plant pot.' Joshua sat Oliver down on a garden seat whilst Billy and Jake looked for the key.

'No plant pots and no key,' said Billy. 'Wot do we do now?' Jake looked up at the back of the house.

'I think that window is open up there. I'm used to climbing. It's how I used to get into the British Library.' He hooked his metal hand around a cast-iron drainpipe and started to climb. Ten minutes later, he opened the back door. 'Even if we had found the key, it wouldn't have been any use because the door was bolted from the inside!' Thirty minutes later, they were all in bed. They had dragged

Oliver up to the attic, where the servants' quarters were, and then each taken a room. It had been an exhausting day with very little to show for their exertions.

Morning came. Joshua returned to The Rookery to escort Charlotte from Cissie's house to their new base. Billy set to work cleaning out the large kitchen range and lit it using coal he found in the cellar. His aim for the day was to cook a stew using the mutton he had bought the previous day. He was pleased to discover there was a herb garden. He couldn't remember if it was mint or parsley he was supposed to use with mutton or what they looked like, so he picked a handful of anything that looked like a herb to enhance his creation. Jake sat at the kitchen table, removed his metal hand, and set to work making some refinements. He had added a new function when they were in Foula, but it needed some adjustments. His hand now had a pressure pad in the palm, and if contact were to be made with sufficient force, his hand would continue to close and not stop until a button was pressed. A second press and the clenched hand would release. He thought that might prove useful when clinging onto a rope. As for Oliver, he slept all morning.

When Joshua arrived to collect Charlotte, he found that Cissie needed him to accompany her on an important errand, a trip to the coffin-makers.

'Please may we borrow a handcart?' asked Cissie, 'Then Joshua here could wheel the coffin home, and tomorrow we can use it to take my brother to St Giles in The Fields Church for his funeral.'

'You certainly can; we've got enough to do 'ere wivout 'aving to traipse about all over The Rookery.'

'I volunteer to prepare your brother's body and place it in the casket,' said Joshua on their way home. 'In my old life, I saw many bodies, from when I was first on the slave ship to when I worked in the fields. I'm not squeamish.'

After everything had been done to prepare for Carrington's funeral, Joshua and Charlotte walked to Baker Street.

'Is Oliver awake yet, Jake?' asked Charlotte. 'I've got something to ask him.'

'Yes, in a manner of speaking,' replied Jake. 'He's up and about, but his brain isn't quite in gear. It needs winding up and he's lost a few cogs! Come through to the kitchen.' Oliver was slumped over a cup of black coffee. He greeted Charlotte, but his voice was a cross between a growl and the noise a kitchen chair makes when dragged across a tiled floor. He kept his head lowered because it hurt to look up, which was just as well as his bloodshot eyes were not a pretty sight.

'Oliver,' began Charlotte, 'I have two things I want to ask you. Please say yes. Firstly, I spent some time with Sadie last night and said I would ask you if she could join us. And before you get any ideas, she wants to retire from her current profession.' Oliver nodded slowly, it was more a case of processing the information than giving an affirmation.

'By all means, the more, the merrier,' he murmured.

'Ha! Yer don't sound very merry,' laughed Billy. Charlotte pressed on.

'And the second thing is Cissie. Now that she doesn't get an allowance from her brother, she is already in arrears with her rent and will end up getting evicted. She has paid for a plot in the cemetery for her brother, and I will talk about the funeral in a minute, but after that, she will have very little savings left and has no desire to stay in The Rookery. I wondered if your brother might like a housekeeper on Foula.' Again Oliver nodded. 'Can I take that as a yes, then?' Oliver continued to nod. 'Going back to Sadie, there will be an element of risk. The gangs control Madame Boo-Boo's now. They won't be happy with you taking away one of their assets.' Oliver didn't have to say anything; Charlotte knew exactly how he felt because when he raised his head, he was smiling, and for the first time that day, there was a twinkle in his eye.

CHAPTER FIFTEEN

The weak morning sun struggled to reach the church of St Giles in the Fields, not even strong enough to cast shadows between the gravestones. Seven figures stood around an open grave as Carrington's coffin was lowered.

'... earth to earth, ashes to ashes, dust to dust; in sure and certain hope of the Resurrection to eternal life,' intoned the vicar. Cissie, Oliver, Charlotte, Jake, Joshua and Billy each took a handful of earth, threw it down onto the casket, and stood in silent reflection. Oliver held up a hand, commanding attention, then began to recite a piece he had memorised from the Bible.

"Behold, I will stretch out mine hand upon the Philistines...And I will execute great vengeance upon them with furious rebukes; and they shall know that I am the

LORD, when I shall lay my vengeance upon them."

Charlotte and Jake looked him full in the eye, but Oliver did not acknowledge them. He gritted his teeth and stared far off into the future.

The madam of the brothel called up the stairs:

'Sooner you get her back on the straight and narrow, the better it will be for her.' Charlotte had made the mistake of calling her Mrs Boo-Boo before, which had been greeted with hoots of laughter.

'There 'aint no such person! My name is Clarice.' Charlotte knocked on Sadie's door.

'It's me. Can I come in?' The key turned in the lock.

'I've got it, Charlotte,' Sadie said excitedly, 'I know when the cannon test will be. See this!'

Charlotte looked at a piece of paper adorned with a military crest.

'What is this?'

'It's a pass you have to show to be allowed into Regent's Park to see the testing. The Major left it in Trixie's room by mistake. I kind of borrowed it when she wasn't looking. He's visiting her tonight, so he's bound to want to collect it then.'

'Do you think I could borrow it?' asked Charlotte.

'As long as you get it back by this evening.'

'I promise I will. Anyway, good news. Oliver is happy for you to join the crew. I checked with him again once his hangover had gone. Will you be ready to come when I return with the pass?'

'I'm not going without all my clothes,' said Sadie.

'I'm sure Joshua will help carry them.' Charlotte went to the window and looked out. Below was a squalid backyard where two cats were fighting on a wall. In the alley beyond, she could hear children kicking a tin can around. Then, further away, was another row of equally depressing houses, dirty curtains fluttering through open windows, a woman pouring slops out of her window, and the sound of a baby crying.

'There's a whole other world than all this, Sadie, and I will be at your side when we take you there.'

'It's good news about the publisher that Jake's friend recommended,' said Charlotte later to Edward. 'When will you get a copy?'

'I'll get a proof tomorrow. Jed Bloxham said he really enjoyed reading it and he won't charge me for this one. He will offset costs for the next one against any profits from the first pamphlet.'

'What's the story about?'

'I've described Joshua's escape from the clutches of slavery. You have to understand that, although they are based on facts, my stories are works of fiction, so I have embellished the tale to make it popular. I know we often joke that Joshua looks like a prince when he wears his cloak, but in my story, he really is one, robbed of his birthright by his evil stepbrother and sold into slavery.'

'Ha ha!' laughed Joshua. 'I look forward to claiming my kingdom! And all I thought I had left behind was a leaky fishing boat!'

'Wot's the story called?' asked Billy, 'Although seein' as I can't read it, it won't make no bleedin' difference t'me.'

'You can't read!' gasped Charlotte, 'Then I will teach you.'

'It's called "Adventures of the Rebel Runaways: A

Princely Bid for Freedom,"'said Edward proudly.

'I like it,' said Billy, '"Rebel Runaways", I proper like it.'

'It's an excellent title because we are all running away from something,' said Charlotte: 'You, Billy from your life as a destitute street urchin in the East End; Jake from life in The Rookery and the Steam Works - a life that disregarded your brilliant engineering mind; Joshua, from slavery and Sadie, when she joins us, will be running away from a life as a prostitute. As for me, I'm running away from a world of privilege that turns a blind eye to the suffering of others in the pursuit of money.'

'What about Oliver?' asked Edward, 'Where is he anyway?'

'Oh! He's gone back to bed. He's running away from all sorts of things. From his former military life and the dark things that happened then, from the expectation that he should return home to manage the family estate that provides him with money, and, not least, he's only ever a few steps away from the clutches of alcohol.'

As they talked, they watched Jake copy the pass that Sadie had 'borrowed'. He was using paper and inks that he had found in the nursery of the Baker Street house. 'I wasn't sure who should use the pass,' said Charlotte, 'It just seemed too good an opportunity to miss.'

'It will be very risky for you, Oliver or me to go to the testing. Given that both Hastings and the soldiers are looking for us, it will be a bit like walking into the lion's den,' said Jake.

'I'd love to have it,' volunteered Edward. 'Not only would I do whatever I could to help, but it gives me the perfect opportunity to write a story for Reuters that might secure my employment. Nobody would connect me to any of you.'

'Perfect!' cried Charlotte. 'That looks finished now, Jake.'

'It's the best I can do with these materials and the time available.'

'I had better get the original back to Madame Boo-Boo's before the Major arrives,' said Charlotte. 'I'm staying at Cissie's again tonight.'

'I shall come with you,' said Joshua, 'Oliver gave me money to pay the toll if we are accosted.'

'I can't tell you how aggrieved Oliver is at the thought of handing over cash to the Black Feathers,' laughed Jake.

'It's time I went home,' said Edward, 'I've finished my next story about defeating a hundred Manchester Scuttler gang members in a bare-knuckle fight that lasted three hours. Then I need to write about our adventures in Bristol, and I have a few ideas for stories I can make up that involve Birmingham and Liverpool.'

'Edward!' gasped Charlotte, 'You are incorrigible!'

'You're back, are you? I'll have to start charging you an entry fee,' cackled Clarice.

'I'm making progress,' replied Charlotte, 'I've persuaded her to go for a walk outside. Show her face, so to speak, now that the swelling has gone down a bit.' Clarice frowned:

'The boys from the gang aren't going to be pleased that our takings have gone down in the last few days; there's plenty of customers who aren't bothered what her face looks like. Mind you get her to see sense!'

'Sympathetic soul,' muttered Charlotte under her breath as she climbed the stairs.

'I'm ready,' said Sadie, 'Have you brought that pass back? Trixie is out at the moment, meeting her Major for tea. Stay here while I slip it back in her room.' She was soon back.

'My, you do have a lot of dresses, don't you,' said Charlotte in surprise.

'I tied them up in one big bundle at first, but then I realised it wouldn't fit through the window, so I've split it into two. I've used my sheets to tie around them. I'm going to burn them later, too many memories! Is Joshua here?'

'He will be,' said Charlotte. 'He forced open the gate from the alley before I came inside.' Charlotte opened the window as wide as it would go, and then the two of them squeezed Sadie's bundles through, knowing that Joshua was poised below to catch them.

'I had a client who liked to buy me dresses, only for me to take 'em off again,' explained Sadie. 'My hairbrush, powder and scent and the like are wrapped up in my clothes, so other than me shawl, there's nowt else I want in this room.'

'Then let's go.'

As they walked down the stairs, Trixie and her Major came through the front door. They waited whilst Sadie and Charlotte descended. Charlotte gasped and turned her head when she saw the soldier. She realised that she recognised him. Luckily he didn't notice her; he was too busy squeezing Trixie's bottom. It was none other than Major Drummond, the very same man that her parents had invited to dinner on the day when her world turned upside down.

Joshua was waiting at the entrance to the alley, and the three of them set off for Cissie's house. For the people they passed, it was an unusual enough sight to see a black man in The Rookery, but what was even more striking was that both the women that accompanied him were beaming with delight.

'How do you fancy helping with my plan, Billy?' asked Jake the following morning.

'Yeah! I'm up for it!'

'Good. But you can't go dressed like a rainbow. I don't suppose you've got any of your old clothes in the den where the airship is moored?'

'Well, I have, actually, but I was hoping not to wear those again. Besides, it's a long way, can't we buy some from around here?'

'I've another reason to go. I want to make some improvements to the airship. I'll go and ask Oliver; we'll need money for the ferry, and I want to buy a brush and a pot of paint, and we may need to pay off the Wild Boys if we come across them.'

'I was that close to catching them, Sir,' whined Hastings. ' I followed them to Birmingham, and I had a report from a train driver that they were in Bristol; they tied up that blasted airship to the new bridge, as bold as brass.'

'It can't be helped,' replied Fotheringay, 'I still want…no, demand, that you catch them, but right now, it's imperative that you are here for the testing of Tiberius. Nothing is more important than demonstrating the effectiveness and superiority of our weapon to the army. If this Hooky fellow is a spy, you must make sure he is not in the vicinity of the testing.'

'And your daughter, Sir?'

'She is no longer my daughter. I have no daughter. Nothing can go wrong. Do you hear me? Nothing!'

Jake handed over his toll money to the Black Feathers who slouched at the entrance to The Rookery.

'D'yer fink we should tell 'em that in the East End, the Wild Boys are chargin' twice as much?' whispered Billy as they walked away. Jake wore his top hat decorated with cogs, a silk scarf and a fancy, embroidered waistcoat. Now that Oliver had sobered up, it was rare for him to return from an excursion without an assortment of new clothes. Shopping had replaced drinking in his life, and he took as much pleasure in dressing up his crew as himself. Or rather, in dressing the male members of the crew. He wasn't sure what to do with Charlotte. She had her own ideas, and he wasn't sure he liked them. So, Jake looked quite the dandy, but Billy looked like a street urchin once again. Jake flipped open the cover on his new silver pocket watch, another gift from Oliver.

'Good, we are on time. The shift change is due soon.' Jake was heading back to the Steam Works but knew not to go in. He couldn't risk it again. On the other hand, Billy was unknown at the Steam Works, and no one took that much notice of kids. 'Are you sure you know what to do?'

'Yeah, I'm sure,' replied Billy. 'I go in wiv the uvver workers and turn left down the first corridor; I ignore the first time it forks but go right at the second one; then at the end is a locker room and 'angin' in a cupboard inside are the apprentice engineers' coats. I find one that fits and then wander abaht a bit, and then when I'm sure no one's around, I 'ide in the back of the broom cupboard and wait until I 'ear an 'ooter that'll mean there's another shift change. Then I come back 'ere, wearin' me coat.'

'Exactly! I'll be here waiting for you. You'll be bored I'm afraid. It will be another three hours before the next set of workers leaves. Get yourself in the middle of them. I'm going to see Old Nick.'

CHAPTER SIXTEEN

'Where are you, Old Nick?'

'Is that you, Jake? I'm back here. Come and join me for a cup of tea and a piece of cake.'

'Cake, eh' said Jake, entering the storeroom where he found Nick sitting on an upturned tea chest, 'Are you celebrating?'

'I most certainly am. I've just been promised some work from the Steam Works. Now, before you say anything, I know things haven't been exactly cordial between you and Fotheringay, but I couldn't say no.'

'Not at all, my friend. You've got a living to make. I'm surprised you've not worked for them before.'

'It's on account of the horse flu. Now that getting deliveries from a distance is difficult, they are looking for more local suppliers and tradesmen. They were too snooty to give out contracts to someone from The Rookery before, but now they need me 'cause I'm the nearest and can sort 'em out in no time. But don't worry, son, I'll always stay loyal to you.'

'That is good news,' replied Jake.

'They said mostly I'll be doing repairs, or going in and dismantling a machine so I can bring a part back and make a new one, but sometimes they might give me new stuff too.'

'Actually, you could be very useful to us in the future. You might be one of the first people to know what they are up to. Oliver has a post office box in Scotland. I can find the address for you. Would you be willing to contact us if you hear of anything we might be interested in?'

'I will be very pleased to be of service, my lad. Have another piece of cake.'

Old Nick couldn't spend the rest of the afternoon eating cake and chatting. He needed to get on with some work, so Jake set off to wait for Billy.

Jake kept a close lookout for gang members who might want to relieve him of 'toll money'. He noticed the tell-tale garb of a youth in a bowler hat with a feather stuck in the band ahead of him and was just about to skirt around another way when he realised he knew the young lady the gang member was arguing with. He quickly approached them and instinctively took off the leather glove hiding his metal hand. He could hear the conversation now:

'I tell you, I've already paid today. You lot are bleeding me dry.'

'Hello Maggie,' said Jake, 'How's the candle-making business? Can I be of any assistance?' He tipped his hat in the way he'd seen Oliver do.

'Hooky!' gasped Maggie.

'Now then,' said the Black Feather, 'Have you come to pay the tolls? One for her and one for you.' Jake found himself copying Oliver's manner too.

'I have already paid an exorbitant sum earlier this afternoon; I am in no mood to pay any more, and I believe the same applies to the good lady here.'

'In no mood, eh! Maybe this will help change your mood!' The youth brandished a long knife, but Jake took a swipe at the blade with his metal hand and it went clattering across the road. The hours spent sparring with Edward on the airship had not been wasted. The youth swung a punch at Jake with his right hand, but Jake was expecting it and easily parried it with his left, then threw a right jab which caught the ruffian full on his nose and made him stagger back. By now, Jake had adopted the boxing stance Edward had taught him.

'I could as easily have hit you with this,' said Jake, shaking his metal hand, 'If that's what you want.' The Black Feather clearly did not want to come into contact with Jake's left fist but seemed unsure how to extricate himself from the situation. 'I suggest that we put it down to a case of mistaken identity, and we go our separate ways,' continued Jake, 'You appear to have dropped your knife. By all means retrieve it, and I may bid you a good day!' Jake remained on his guard in case the youth grabbed the knife and lunged at him, but he didn't; he grabbed it and ran a few steps to put some distance between them, then attempted to swagger down the road as though nothing had happened.

'Oh, Hooky! Just look at you! You've done well for yourself.'

'Allow me to walk you home,'

'By all means.'

'Actually, no offence, but no one calls me Hooky any more. My friends all call me by my name - Jake. Anyway, as you can see. I don't have a hook any more.'

'I can't believe it's you, Jake. You were always so shy with the girls.'

'I was never shy with you, Maggie. You always gave me the time of day. I'll never forget that.'

'I'm surprised such a gent as yourself can be bothered to associate themselves with the likes of me.'

'Underneath these fine clothes, I'm still me, Maggie. It's just that I wasn't allowed to flourish in the past, but I've met some good people, and everything has changed. So how is business for you?'

'Oh, Jake! It's terrible. So many houses are closed up that it's hard to find people to sell to, and then, as you saw, the gangs want to take more and more. The trouble with walking the streets to sell candles is that I venture into lots of different territories, so it's not just the Black Feathers I have to contend with; it's The Wild Boys and The Golden-Lane gang and more. If it weren't for the fact that our Freddie is old enough to work now, we'd be destitute.'

'How much would the candles in your basket cost?'

'I was hoping to get another five shillings for these.'

'In that case, I will buy them from you. We ought to replace the ones we have been burning here in London. I will have a word with my friend; it's his money, really. It could well be that he would be happy to buy a box to take back to…to…no, it will be better for your sake if I don't tell you where we are going next.'

'I understand, Jake. I know the soldiers were looking for you. Mind you, they seem to have stopped lately.'

'If all goes to plan, they will soon start to look for me

again.'

Before Billy and Jake returned to Baker Street, they called in to see Sadie and Charlotte at Cissie's house so Jake could give them an outline of the plan. Charlotte couldn't help smiling at the scowl on Billy's face. She was so used to him dressing like a gaudy peacock, yet here he was in his urchin's rags wearing a dusty brown engineer's overall. Once the boys had left, the conversation about fashion continued.

'I don't know the best way to say this, Charlotte, but I don't really understand your style of clothes,' said Sadie, carefully.

'You must remember what I was wearing that first time we met, Sadie. It was in the fashion that the society I lived in found acceptable for women. All those buttons and bows and ribbons and pretty-pretty fabrics. I've left that behind now.'

'Of course I remember that dress; I still have it. Only I reckoned you wouldn't ever want it back, so I adapted it. Look!' Sadie reached into the pile of dresses on the bed and pulled out a garment. Charlotte recognised the fabric, but the shape was completely different. 'I cut away that high neck so you can see my corset and raised the hem at the front so you can see my legs,' said Sadie proudly.

'Goodness! But I wouldn't want to look like a…a…a'

'A tart! I know, because I am one. No! I was one! But surely there's got to be somewhere in the middle? I appreciate your clothes might be practical for flying an airship, but it's like you're hiding away. You should be proud you are a woman.'

'I am! Well, I'm proud that I can fly an airship.'

'How hard can that be?'

'You'd be surprised! I am probably the only female pilot in Great Britain, perhaps the world. But I don't know how to translate that into fashion.'

'You have to realise how I dressed as a tart gave me power. It meant I could manipulate the men. What they saw through their eyes went straight to their heart…and other parts of their body,' Sadie added with a laugh, 'It certainly didn't go to their brains. Jake needs you to be successful on Monday, and you need a helping hand from your clothes.'

'I know, it's a bit of a worry,' agreed Charlotte.

'It needn't be. I would do it, but with a face as battered and bruised as mine is at the moment, it wouldn't work. Talking of Jake, I think he's got a decent style. All those cogs decorating his hat!'

'I've got a top hat too.'

'Well, you should wear it. When you look back at what Jake used to look like, he made hardly any impression at all. I used to see him sometimes in The Rat talking to Old Nick. I'm used to checking out the men in case there might be some business coming my way. The only things to notice about Jake were that he wouldn't make eye contact, was drinking milk, and had a hook for a hand, which he tried to keep hidden away. Now, look at him!'

'He still drinks milk but is very proud of his new hand. He tends to keep it hidden by wearing gloves when we are in The Rookery, but normally he keeps it polished and visible. He's always tinkering with it to make improvements.'

'It's as though what runs through the heart of him, engineering and all that, is worn on the outside. In fact, that's a good word. Outside. We want to be 'outsiders,' said

Sadie.

'You've convinced me. It's time to rip it all up and start again. Outsiders! That gives me an idea. Why don't I wear one of your black corsets on the outside? Like a waistcoat. It'll still be mixing the masculine and the feminine, but with a bit more dash.'

'Perfect! And lots of petticoats and high boots. That will disarm them!'

'You're right. Thank you, Sadie.'

'See! I'm not just a pretty face!'

'Well, you're not even that at the moment!' and the two dissolved into laughter.

'Do you know what we need?' said Charlotte later as they sorted through the pile of Sadie's dresses for the ones they intended to deconstruct, 'My Singer.'

'A singer! You have someone to serenade you when you work?'

'No, it's a sewing machine.'

'I didn't know there was such a thing.'

'They are new. They were invented in America, and now they are made in Glasgow as well. They are very expensive, and there's one sitting in my study. It was a birthday present.'

'Well, if it's yours, why don't we get it?'

'We shall! We'll need Joshua, though. It weighs a ton!.

Charlotte was so nervous that her heart was pounding. She felt more scared than at any time since she had witnessed Hastings' murderous attack on Carrington. Thinking of that horrible event gave her the courage to open the gate to her family home and sneak around to the tradesman's entrance, followed by Sadie, Joshua and Jake.

Jake was intrigued by the idea of a machine that could sew and couldn't wait to take it to bits to see how it worked. Although Charlotte's parents were at home they were creatures of habit, so she knew where they would be. The friends waited out of sight. Jake checked his pocket watch, then, on the stroke of seven, a gong sounded. It was the signal that dinner was being served. A little later, the back door opened, just as Charlotte expected, and a hot and rotund cook emerged to cool off outside.

'Hello, Cookie,' whispered Charlotte.

'Charlotte, where have you been?' Charlotte put a finger to her lips.

'Shush! Read this. I'm in it!' Charlotte handed Cookie a copy of Edward's newly printed story, "Rebel Runaways". 'I'm not coming back. Don't tell Mother and Father I've been. I've just come to collect my sewing machine.' Charlotte embraced the cook as she did every one of the other servants she met on the way to her old study.

Later that evening, when Charlotte's mother came down to the kitchen to complain that the fish had been overcooked, she caught one of the maids hastily stuffing Edward's pamphlet under her apron. Mrs Fotheringay held out her hand for the book.

'Rebel Runaways,' she read, 'Really, Gladys! Can't you read something more cultural? Something more appropriate for this household. What would people think?'

CHAPTER SEVENTEEN

'Good morning, Fotheringay. Is everything on track for tomorrow?'

'Yes, Field Marshal. It's all going very smoothly. We have cordoned off the area around Regent's Park and have armed sentries at every entrance. Anyone wishing to enter the park must show a pass,' replied Fotheringay.

'A lot is riding on this. The next logical step will be to use it on the battlefield, so it has to go well. What's the power source?'

'Steam, of course. We are conducting experiments into constructing portable compressed steam canisters, but that's for the future. One of our pipelines goes through Regent's Park, so we shall tap into that.'

'And how are you transporting Tiberius to the park?

When I saw it in your factory, it looked very cumbersome.'

'We are making use of the new prisoner labour force. They aren't as manageable as horses, but with enough of them, they can pull anything. Maybe we have to whip them a little more than we used to whip the horses, but that's the only encouragement they understand.'

'God knows there's no shortage of inmates. The prisons are overflowing. Sometimes I think the gaolers hope a few will try to escape so we can shoot them and create some more room.'

'What about this Hooky fellow? Any developments there?'

'We were on his trail but it went cold. We won't give up, but I don't think he's a problem. I understand that government spies in our potential enemy countries have had no word of any liaison with him, so if he is working alone there's no great threat.

Jake was walking down the stairs in the Baker Street house that morning when he was surprised to hear a key turning in the lock of the front door. The Runaways had never used that door themselves as they only had a key to the back door. Jake paused, unsure about what to do. After all, it wasn't his house and, therefore, not his place to determine who entered it. The door opened to reveal a middle-aged man. He didn't look like a house owner; more like an upper servant, going by his clothes.

'Hello, my name is Jake; I'm here with Oliver.'

'Aagh!' the man was visibly shocked to encounter anyone.

'So sorry. I didn't mean to surprise you. Can I make you a cup of tea?' Now the man was confused. His first thought was probably that Jake must be a burglar, but an offer of a drink was not the response he might have expected.

'Who…who…who are you?' he stammered, 'What are you doing here?'

'As I said, I'm Jake, Jake Moss, and I'm here as a guest with Oliver Moon.'

'Confound it! Who on earth is Oliver Moon?'

'Oliver's a friend of Bertram.'

'Dash it all! Who is Bertram?'

'He lives here.'

'He most certainly does not. I've worked here all my life, and no one of that name has ever lived here.'

'Perhaps you had better speak to Oliver. He's in the kitchen.' Now they were both confused. 'Oliver, allow me to introduce you to…sorry, I don't know your name.'

'It's Silverson. I am the butler here.' If Silverson had been shocked to find a young man with a metal hand in the hallway, he was even more shocked to find a tall black man sitting at the kitchen table and a young boy stirring the pot that was bubbling on the range, as well as the dapper yet somewhat eccentric man who jumped up to shake his hand.

'Pleased to meet you. Is Bertram coming back to London?"

'Who on earth is Bertram?' cried the exasperated Silverson.

It took a full fifteen minutes for everyone to deduce that they should have been staying a Two Baker Street, not Twenty-Two.

'Ah! I do apologise. An honest mistake,' said Oliver. 'And we only had one more night to stay.'

Just then, they heard a loud hammering on the door. Silverson turned to go and answer it. Something about the urgency of the noise made Jake, Oliver and Joshua follow him. They stood to one side as Silverson opened the door.

'Just an 'ouse call, my friend,' came a very uncultured voice, 'It's time we was collecting the local taxes.'

'I think you are mistaken; you also must have the wrong house. Good morning to you,' replied Silverson, attempting to close the door. Jake flattened himself against the wall. This visitor sounded very much like a street-gang member, an impression reinforced when a boot was thrust out to prevent the door from closing.

'No, it's you who are mistaken, my friend. Maybe this will clear up any confusion.' Silverson found himself with a knife pointing at his throat. Jake acted instinctively and leapt forward, slamming his hand against the assailant's wrist. The mechanism he had recently perfected worked brilliantly because his hand immediately clenched and continued to squeeze tighter and tighter. The intruder made a noise of surprise at first, then yelled in pain as the pressure increased, giving him no option other than to drop the knife. Jake pressed a button to stop his fist from tightening further, and he twisted, forcing the gang member to the floor. Another man burst in. If he had entered more cautiously he might have noticed Joshua standing just inside the doorway, but instead he found himself in a bear hug. Joshua was behind him, and his powerful arms were exerting nearly as much pressure as Jake's metal hand. Another knife clattered to the floor.

Meanwhile, Oliver, with a bemused smile, strode across the vestibule. He had previously admired the crossed swords mounted on the wall beneath a heraldic crest and lifted one down.

'Allow me, Mr Silverson,' he said, gently moving the transfixed butler aside, so he could greet a third gang member, who was standing on the doorstep, with a welcoming smile, while gently waving the sword at him.

'I can make it go tighter,' warned Jake.

'No, no, no,' screamed his assailant.

'I can make spikes shoot through into your arteries,' continued Jake. This was a bluff, as his hand had no such feature.

'Permit me to outline the situation,' said Oliver calmly. 'One of you is in danger of losing his hand, another of receiving several cracked ribs, and you outside are intact…for the moment. However, I think my sword would be capable of removing several limbs. I'm spoiled for choice! I conclude that it would now be prudent for you to withdraw in the knowledge that this house falls under the protection of…The Rebels.'

The man held by Joshua was now suspended several inches off the floor. He nodded furiously.

'Yes, Yes,' screamed the man held in Jake's grip. 'Let me go!'

'I seem to remember,' said Silverson to Jake once their visitors had scrambled away and the door had been shut, 'That you offered me a cup of tea. One more night, you say. I'm sure I can sanction that.'

Before moving to Scotland, Cissie had a list of neighbours she wanted to visit.

'Thank you for offering to come with me,' she said to Charlotte and Sadie, 'I've got too many ornaments to carry by myself, and it means I can give them to my friends at the same time as saying goodbye.'

'Glad to help,' replied Charlotte, warmly.

'There's no point leaving them behind,' added Sadie,

'As soon as the kids realise your house is empty, they will break in and smash everything up just for the fun of it.'

'And these baskets of food will be appreciated. The rats won't take long to move into my kitchen.'

'Makes me shudder just to think about it,' said Charlotte.

'Oh, you get used to rats living in The Rookery. I need to square my rent with the landlord, then one more night to sleep in London.'

'And you will be off to start your new life,' said Charlotte.

'To be honest, I'm a bit nervous. I've only ever lived in London. The biggest expanse of green I've ever seen is Hyde Park. I can't imagine being somewhere so isolated as the island you described, Charlotte.'

Eventually, they finished Cissie's errands and set off home.

'Your swelling has gone down a lot, Sadie,' said Charlotte, linking arms with her friend.

'I can at least see out of both eyes, although these black rings around them aren't exactly pretty. Oh no!' Sadie froze. In the street ahead were six gang members, Black Feathers, pointing at her. They ran towards her and quickly surrounded her, grabbing her by the arms. She screamed, and they laughed.

'Your little holiday is over. You are coming with us.'

'Leave her!' shouted Charlotte. She remembered the little gun that Oliver had given her. How stupid to have left it behind!

'Stay out of it, you. Or we'll carve you up!' Then they dragged poor, struggling Sadie down the road.

'I'll follow them,' said Cissie to Charlotte. She had been walking a little way behind the two girls, having stopped to chat with a friend. 'I'm just an old woman; they won't notice me. Sometimes it's like I'm invisible. You go home; I'll see you later.'

Cissie had an idea where they might be heading, and she was right. It was a three-storey inn called 'The Executioner', and for some years now it had served as the headquarters of The Black Feathers. No sane person who was not one of the gang would ever venture in there. It was renowned for fights between tetchy, hard-drinking gang members. They wouldn't take too kindly to strangers venturing onto their territory. Cissie didn't immediately return home. She waited and watched. Eventually, she was rewarded because a figure appeared in an attic room window. She knew it was Sadie by the colour of her clothes. She waved, but she had no idea if Sadie saw her.

Jake and Joshua brought more clothes round to Cissie's house - including Oliver's latest purchases - so all the luggage was in one place. The airship would call by, piloted by Oliver with Jake and Joshua as crew, to pick everything up in the morning. The most awkward item would be the sewing machine.

Jake and Joshua were shocked when Charlotte told them what had happened to Sadie.

'I know it's hard, but you must concentrate on what you have to do in the morning. You know Sadie would want you to do your part well,' said Jake.

'But we can't leave her,' wailed Charlotte.

'And we won't. But we can't do anything about it tonight,' insisted Jake, 'You must come to Baker Street at eight o clock in the morning to meet up with Billy and Edward. It's only about a ten-minute walk from there to Regent's Park. Oliver, Joshua and I will have already left to collect the airship. Cissie will stay here until we arrive. I promise you we won't abandon Sadie. I've one more job to do, and that's to collect a big box of candles from my friend, Maggie, and then Joshua and I will walk over to take a look at The Executioner.

CHAPTER EIGHTEEN

Jake was the navigator, a fairly easy task as it was just a case of heading East from Blackwall, past Tower Bridge, then Oliver tweaked the airship a few degrees northwards. Soon they were flying over St Giles-in-the-Fields Church, where Jake could see the mound of earth where Carrington had been laid to rest, and then on to The Rookery.

'There! That's Cissie's house,' Jake shouted. Oliver kept the airship hovering above it whilst Joshua descended on the rope ladder. Very quickly, a crowd of urchins and beggars gathered outside the house, watching removals such as they had never seen before. Cissie carried items out, Joshua placed them in a large basket tied to a rope, and Jake winched it up to the airship. They had to bring things outside individually, or their audience would soon whisk them away. They left the two trickiest items until last. The first was the sewing machine, which, with its cast iron treadle base, was very heavy, and the second was Cissie herself.

'Who would have thought I would be dangling in the air at my ripe old age?' marvelled Cissie, halfway up the ladder.

'Can anyone read?' shouted Jake once Cissie was bundled inside the gondola. Only a handful of people in the assembled crowd put up their hands. Jake shimmied down the ladder and handed out Edward's "Rebel Runaways" stories. 'Read them to the others and pass them on. This one features Joshua here.' The former slave duly performed an extravagant bow. 'There will be more stories to come. Look out for them.' Oliver had ensured that there would be a second print run because, unbeknown to Edward, he had purchased several boxes of the story books and stacked them on the airship. He determined to distribute free copies in every city or town they visited.

As the airship began to glide away, Cissie looked down on the house she had lived in for so long, but she did not shed any tears. It didn't particularly hold happy memories; first, her husband had died there, and then her brother. She had always felt under siege from the thieves and robbers outside. At the age of sixty, which in The Rookery was a rare milestone, she felt it was time to turn the page to a new chapter in her life.

'Now to rescue Sadie,' said Jake. 'Onwards to The Executioner.'

'It's still early,' said Oliver, 'These gangs are not renowned for being early risers. They will have been drinking until late. I actually know that pub from the days before Crusty Jack revoked my amnesty. I must stay on board to keep the airship flying, but I can describe the layout.'

Jake and Joshua descended to the street outside the pub a few moments later.

'I bet you the door is open,' said Jake. 'After all, who would try and rob a gang's stronghold?' Joshua turned the handle and eased the door open. They paused and listened. Silence. Then they slipped inside. It took a few moments for their eyes to adjust. They were in the main bar; there were no curtains or shutters, but in any case the windows were so dirty that very little light filtered through. Joshua and Jake picked their way between the shadowy forms of sleeping gang members; several had half-drunk glasses of beer in front of them. Jake put his finger to his lips, a rather pointless gesture as they both knew they must not make a sound. Ahead of them was the doorway which Oliver had told them led to the stairs, and they crept over to it. Luckily, the door was ajar, and they started to climb, praying that the stairs didn't creak.

Suddenly, they were faced with a growling bull terrier staring at them from the top of the stairs. The dog was white with eyes of fiery red, then a brindled companion appeared at its side and both dogs began to bark.

'Shuddup!' came a shout from upstairs. A moment later, the two dogs rushed at Jake and Joshua. They didn't look like the kind of dogs one would want to pet! Jake and Joshua half fell, half slid down the stairs and tumbled through the doorway. Jake slammed the door shut, and the two dogs crashed against it, snarling and yelping. The friends spun around to see that everyone in the bar was now awake. There was a pause, only punctuated by the noise of the dogs.

'Run!' yelled Jake, and he and Joshua dashed out of

the pub. 'There!' shouted Jake, pointing to the dangling rope ladder. Joshua got there first and leapt to grab hold of it, followed by Jake, who just managed to get his foot on the bottom rung before hearing Cissie scream:

'Up! Up!' She had been watching from the open doorway of the airship. A few seconds later, the roaring, cursing gang members burst onto the street, ready to do battle with the intruders. Unsurprisingly, the one way they didn't look, as they scattered in all directions, was upwards, and the airship was soon hidden by the clouds.

'It's a good job I'm not scared of heights,' panted Jake as he scrambled aboard. 'How much time have we got before we have to go to Regent's Park, Oliver, so that we can try again?'

'About an hour.'

'It would be madness to go back down there!' said Joshua.

'No, far from it. They won't be expecting us to return. But we can't enter from the bottom and go up. We'll have to go in from above.'

'Good thinking, Jake,' said Oliver, 'We must use the fact that we are in an airship to our advantage.'

'I noticed the pub roof is made of overlapping slates. If we remove a few, we can climb down into the attic. Let's wait until they have all gone back in. I think some rope and an axe is all we will need,' continued Jake.

Five minutes later, Jake and Joshua returned to The Executioner, only this time they sat astride the ridge tiles on the roof, close to a chimney stack. The airship had risen back into the sky, but Cissie was lying on her stomach, looking out of the door with a spyglass to await their signal. Jake and Joshua were not unduly worried about being spotted.

'The street outside is so narrow that no one from the pub could stand back far enough to see us up here,' chuckled Joshua.

'Anyone looking from the top windows of the houses opposite could see us,' replied Jake, 'But we'll just have to take our chances with that.'

'I doubt the gang are the best of neighbours, so people probably won't care, anyway.'

'We'll start there,' said Jake, pointing to a spot below them. 'Tie the rope around the chimney stack, Joshua; this roof looks steep and slippy!' With his metal hand clutching the rope, Jake slid down the roof, inserted the axe beneath one of the slates, and then jerked it upwards. It snapped in half. He threw the broken slate to Joshua, who placed it on the chimney stack. He repeated this process with the adjoining three slates. Now that a row of slates below the broken ones was exposed, he could easily remove it and then the row below. Kneeling on the rafters, he swung the axe against the laths that spanned them until he had exposed a hole big enough for them both to wriggle through. Jake lowered the rope and entered the loft space, followed by Joshua. He knew he was directly above the room where Cissie had seen Sadie.

'Make sure you step on the ...' Too late. Before Jake could say the word 'rafters', Joshua disappeared from view with a crash, accompanied by a scream from the room below. Jake peered through the hole in the ceiling. Joshua was sitting on a pile of broken laths on the floor. Sadie was open-mouthed on the bed, and both were white with plaster dust.

'Hello, Sadie,' said Jake cheerfully, 'Are you alright?'

'Ecky Thump! You two certainly know how to make an entrance!' she said with a nervous laugh.

'Come on,' said Jake urgently, dropping the end of the rope into the room. 'Let's get out of here in case anyone heard us. The airship is coming to collect us.'

'No, wait!' There's a lass in the next room. She sounds really young, and she keeps crying for her ma. The gang said there would be some kind of initiation ceremony tomorrow. That doesn't sound good.'

'I'll lift you up, Sadie. Grab hold of that rope, and then I will go and look,' replied Joshua.

Moments later, Joshua kicked at the lock, breaking it; the door swung open, and he was out on the landing. He could hear sounds from the floor below and wondered if anyone had heard the noise. He presumed the adjoining door would be locked so he didn't even try the handle and barged into it with his shoulder. The frame splintered and the door fell flat on the floor. He saw a young girl pressed into a corner. There was no time to explain. Joshua picked her up and carried her struggling, kicking and screaming into the other room. By now, gang members were rushing up the stairs. Joshua crouched, poised at the top, and when the first man reached him, he grasped his arm and leg, straightened up, and threw him back the way he had come to scatter the pursuers tumbling down the stairs like skittles.

Joshua ran back into Sadie's room and saw Jake dangling half out of the hole in the ceiling, trying unsuccessfully to encourage the young girl to climb up the rope. Joshua took matters into his own hands, quite literally, and dragging the bed beneath the hole, he picked the girl up, stood on the bed, and passed her over his head into Jake's outstretched hands. Joshua could hear shouting on the landing, and he pushed the bed against the door, then realising the room wasn't very wide, he sat down with his back against the opposite wall and his feet jammed against the bed. The gang members pounded on the door for several minutes, but there was no possibility of them breaking it down. Joshua gave it a few more minutes to allow Jake to persuade the young girl, now shocked into silence, to climb out onto the roof.

'It's no use! You'll have to come out sometime,' yelled someone from outside the door.

'I can wait,' shouted Joshua. However, he was already scrambling up the rope. He pulled himself up onto the tiles to see Sadie disappearing into the gondola. 'You go next,' Joshua said to Jake. 'Now you.' he said to the stunned girl. If she had been surprised by the sight of a dusty black man crashing into her room, she was absolutely astounded by the huge airship hovering above. Only now did she realise she was being rescued and not trapped in some fearful nightmare. 'Go!' Joshua shouted.

'Don't look down. Look at me!' encouraged Jake. With trembling hands, she began to climb, followed by Joshua. Oliver waited until everyone was aboard before flying away. Looking down, Joshua noticed that no one had followed them onto the roof, and he chuckled at the thought of the Black Feathers waiting outside the bedroom door for him to come out.

'If you want to look like an African prince again, Joshua, you will need a wash,' laughed Jake. 'You look more like an African ghost!'

Cissie rocked the sobbing young girl in her arms.

'What's your name, love?' she asked.

'Ruby. I want to go home.'

'I'm sure we can take you there,' replied Cissie, 'But first of all, we have to go to Regent's Park.'

CHAPTER NINETEEN

'Hello, boys,' said Charlotte to the four soldiers guarding the open wrought iron gate which led into the park.

'Aye, aye!' said one with a leer. Charlotte smiled, tipped her hat coquettishly and kissed the rose she was holding.

'Oh, I do like a man in uniform,' she said, 'I can't think which of you handsome young men I should give my flower to!' If Charlotte had hoped they would see this as a euphemism for something else, she had succeeded. As she swayed her hips and minced along, she drew the men unwittingly away from the open gate. 'Now, you've got nice long legs. I've got long legs, too, see!' She raised her petticoats a few inches. The soldiers nodded in approval.

'But I do like the shape of your mouth,' she said to another. 'Mouths are so important, don't you think?' and she puckered her lips. It took all her restraint not to burst out laughing at the sight of the four soldiers all involuntarily puckering too. She noticed Billy approaching the entrance. The soldiers had their backs to him, but one of them heard him and turned his head.

'Oy!'

'I'm wiv the Steam Works,' replied Billy, 'I gotta deliver this, s'important!' and he walked on confidently. That satisfied the soldier because he had seen other engineers working on the Tiberius cannon earlier that morning wearing similar coats. In any case, Charlotte was now touching his face, which brought the soldier's attention fully back to her.

'Oh! And you've got cute little freckles on your nose. I 'ain't got freckles, but I've got a little mole. I'm not tellin' you where it is, though. You'll have to look for it.'

'Don't mind if I do, my girl!' Charlotte noticed Edward slip through the gates. He was also spotted by one of the soldiers.

'Hey! Where's your pass!' Edward was prepared. In one hand, he held his pocket watch; in the other was Jake's forged pass. He knew it wouldn't bear close scrutiny, so, as he held it up, he broke into a trot.

'Running a bit late,' he shouted, now holding up his pocket watch. 'Must dash!'

'But…' Charlotte was ready for this moment and began to caress the soldier's neck.

'What a fine, strong neck you have. People say I have a beautiful neck. Would you like me to undo a few buttons to show you?' Any thoughts of checking Edward's pass evaporated as Charlotte undid her top button. She had her fingers on the second button when she heard a shout and froze. She knew that voice!

'Hey! What are you doing? Chase that harlot away!' shouted Hastings. Charlotte couldn't help herself. She put her hands on her hips.

'Who are you calling a harlot, you stupid imbecile!' She spun on her heel and sashayed back towards Baker Street. She had done her work.

'Who does he think he is? He's not our commanding officer,' grumbled one of the soldiers. Hastings stared uneasily after the girl. He wouldn't usually care what a streetwalker thought of him, so he couldn't think why he was left feeling troubled.

Billy strode into Regent's Park feeling pleased, both that Charlotte's part of the plan had gone so well and that he was in the midst of the crowd heading towards the park's centre. He was astonished when he finally saw the Tiberius cannon.

'Blimey! It's a lot bigger than I fort it would be,' he said to himself. Jake had sketched the cannon and marked where Billy should place the sign, so before he went any further, Billy checked that he could identify the correct position. Now was not the time to reveal any hesitation. Then, when he felt ready, he plucked up his courage and ducked under the rope that cordoned off the gun.

'Hey!' shouted a guard.

'I won't be a moment!' replied Billy as he tore away the brown paper that hid the metal sign, making sure it faced the crowd of spectators. He gave the soldier a reassuring wave, although he felt far from calm. Jake had instructed him to keep the sign close to his body so no one would notice that there were far more magnets than needed to fix the sign to the cannon. Once the sign was in place, Billy ducked back under the rope.

'That's clever, the way it sticks on,' said the guard.

'Yes, well, it would be bloomin' dangerous to drill into it on account of the 'igh internal pressures,' said Billy, succeeding in sounding knowledgeable. At that moment, two other people ducked under the rope. Although Billy did not realise it, they were Field Marshal Bellings and Fotheringay. The latter noticed the sign; Billy's heart skipped a beat, but Fotheringay just nodded in approval. A photographer with a plate camera mounted on a tripod took a photograph whilst the factory owner and the military government leader posed in front of the sign and shook hands.

Billy felt a strong hand on his shoulder. He spun around to be confronted by a man wearing an engineer's overall identical to his own.

'What are you doing here?' demanded the engineer.

'I was sent to deliver summink, Guv'ner,' stammered Billy.

'And have you?'

'Yes, Sir.'

'Well, then it's time you got back to the Steam Works. I've been told to return, so I don't see why you should stay here. In fact, I will walk back with you. I know just what you apprentices are like; you would be dawdling and sneaking off to buy buns. Come on.'

'Actually,' thought Billy, 'That's exactly what I had planned to do,' but he just nodded and fell into step with the engineer. His every instinct told him to run, but he knew he couldn't. It would draw attention to the fact that he was an interloper, and Jake's plan might fail. Billy was relieved that the engineer was not the chatty type. However, after walking for five minutes, the man spoke:

'I've not seen you before.'

No, Guv'ner. I'm fairly new.' The engineer was puzzled and wondered why a new apprentice would be trusted with a mission to deliver an item on such an important day. Surely a more senior person should have come.

'Who's your supervisor?' Billy was prepared for this question. Jake had given him a name.

'Mr Grimes, Sir,' replied Billy confidently. The man stopped, looked hard at Billy, then seized him by the collar.

'The thing is, there is only one engineer called Grimes, and that's me! I'll be dashed if I'm your supervisor. We will see what Hastings has to say about this!' Grimes started dragging Billy back towards Regent's Park.

Unbeknown to either of them, Jake was tracking their movements through his spyglass.

'Oh no!' he cried. 'They've got Billy. Oliver, how much time do we have?'

'About fifteen minutes.'

'And how long would it take us to get to the river and back.'

'Maybe, ten minutes.'

'Good, can you set Joshua down on the ground nearer the park, around the bend? I'll stay at the bottom of the ladder.' He quickly gave Joshua more instructions, and then they raced to try and save Billy and rescue their plan from failure.

'Gerroff, gerroff. You're hurtin' me!' yelled Billy.

'Shut up, you little tyke!' growled Grimes. As much as Billy struggled, he couldn't break free. He was close to tears thinking that if the plan failed, it would be his fault. Then he relaxed because a big muscular black man was walking towards them with a beaming smile. Grimes ignored Joshua as he passed by, but that wasn't possible a moment later because he found himself being squeezed so tightly that he had to let go of the boy. Then he felt a change of grip, and he was hoisted up higher, while something was thrust down his collar. The hands holding him let go, but he didn't drop to the ground. The opposite happened. He went up.

Billy's mood switched from abject misery to glee, for he had witnessed the whole sequence of events, from Joshua grabbing Grimes and then holding him up to Jake, who was hanging upside down with his legs securely wrapped around the rope ladder like a trapeze artist, to Jake inserting his metal hand inside Grimes' collar and then making his fist clench. Now he delighted in the sight of the struggling engineer flying through the air, away from Regent's Park.

'Come,' said Joshua. 'They will return for us. In the meantime, there is a coffee shop nearby where Charlotte will be waiting.'

'Hello, Mr Grimes,' said Jake, 'I would suggest you don't look down. We really are quite high now. And I would also suggest you don't wriggle around so much. If your collar were to tear, then that would be the end of you.' It dawned on Grimes who the upside-down figure was.

'Hooky! It's you.'

'You know, Mr Grimes. I never cared for that name. I might feel inclined to let go. I always did find you rather rude.'

'No, no, please don't! I'll call you whatever you want.'

'Well, I would prefer it if you called me by my name.'

'But, but, I don't know what it is.'

'That's exactly what I mean! I have known you all my

adult life, and you haven't even bothered to learn my name. It's Jake Moss.'

'I'm sorry, Jake.'

'I think calling me Jake denotes a lack of respect. I would have accepted Mr Moss. I think I might let go after all.'

'No, no, Aagh….' Grimes' scream was cut short as he hit the shallow water by the far bank of the Thames. After spending the terrifying journey looking up at Jake, he hadn't realised that the airship had slowly been descending, and when Jake let go, he only had about twenty feet to fall. Even in the days when there were still horses alive, it would have taken him a long while to get back to the park, but right now, he had no desire to do any such thing. He waded until he found steps leading up from the water, sat on the topmost one, and wept.

198

CHAPTER TWENTY

As the airship flew towards Regent's Park, Sadie reached over and held Ruby's hand to comfort her. Sadie smiled to herself, taking stock of the situation:

'Well, this is a reet adventure. I've barely had time to think. It might be out of the fryin' pan and into the fire, but I don't reckon so. If I've done one good thing it was saving Ruby from the sort of life I had been leading - a life I've no intention of going back to. The Runaways are a grand bunch. Even Oliver, 'cause I must say, I had my concerns havin' got to know him in a different way, if you know what I mean. Mind you, he were always so bladdered that I wonder if he can remember owt about it! It's dead funny to think that I've no idea what I'll be doin' next week. I've spent so much time as a workin' lass, where despite all the different lads, every day and night were pretty much the same, that I feel a bit scared by it all. I mean, I

knew that business, but I've no idea if I can do owt else. I kinda drifted into that game. I mean, back in Manchester I'd had, I'll call 'em 'experiences', from a young age, not o' my askin', but I won't dwell on them times; they weren't happy, and then when I got chucked out of the family home, I came to London and thought I may as well get paid for what had been happenin' to me anyway. But I'm optimistic. Who'd have thought that I could ever have a friend like Charlotte? If she can walk away from her previous life, then so can I! By heck, I'm looking forward to being part of what happens next!'

Edward had seen Billy place the sign on the cannon but hadn't seen the events that transpired afterwards. He had been intrigued by the fact that a photographer was in the park, as he was under the impression that the press were banned from attending this top-secret event. Apart from himself and the photographer, only members of the new government, senior government administrators and high-ranking soldiers were present. Edward waited for the crowd to thin out before talking to the man with the camera.

'Are you working for one of the newspapers?'

'No, I was personally employed by Mr Fotheringay. He wants a photograph for his office.'

'Could I pay you to take a photograph or two for me? Perhaps one when they fire the gun, and also another one I have in mind.'

I'm not sure.'

'How much is he paying you?'

'Five pounds,' replied the photographer proudly.

'I'll pay you double that. For each photograph.'

'But what if Fotheringay finds out I have sold photographs to someone else?'

'Did Fotheringay say you couldn't take any more photos?'

'Well, no. He didn't.'

'In that case, you could always say that your studio was broken into and someone stole the plates. Perhaps an extra five pounds would take care of the inconvenience. And your name is?'

'Daniel Mathers' They shook hands on the deal and exchanged business cards. It was a lot of money, and Edward could only just afford it. However, it was more important that he secured a job with Reuters. He had to think long-term.

'Might I suggest you set up your camera a little further away?'

'I can get a good shot from here.'

'Believe me, a long shot will be best. And can your camera point up in the air?'

'I get it, you want a photo of all the birds taking flight, frightened by this new weapon. Is it going to be noisy?'

'It might well be. Come, let's set up your camera further away.'

Edward and Daniel spent the next twenty minutes watching the army trying to marshal the spectators. Most people wanted to stand where they could see both the cannon and the distant red flag which was the target. The soldiers had announced that the gun would only fire empty glass canisters, so there was no danger. Edward begged to differ, but he was not in a position to say otherwise. At least no one was permitted to stand close to the cannon.

Finally, everything was ready. Hastings opened the valve connecting Tiberius to the steam line. Fotheringay strode imperiously over to the cannon and pulled a lever before returning to join the Field Marshal and the official government party.

'It will be two minutes, precisely,' he announced.

Edward was the only one in the park who knew the proceedings were being watched from a distance, by the audience in the airship. Jake had his telescope trained on Tiberius.

'I don't understand what's happening,' complained Ruby.

'We are trying to prevent that beastly, cowardly gun from working,' said Oliver.

'But how?'

'Let me explain,' said Jake, 'The gun contains a series of cogs and gears, increasing in size, potentially generating considerable power and projecting missiles a long, long way. However most of the workings inside are made of ferromagnetic materials such as iron and steel. In addition, I know from the notes I made in the factory that they are using a highly inflammable lubricant that couldn't be used with gunpowder, but they think it's safe because they are using steam and…'

'Too technical, Jake,' said Charlotte with a laugh, 'You are bamboozling the poor girl. Put simply, Billy put a sign on it, held in place by lots of magnets, which will slow the workings down. It will get hot and in the end, it might melt, or explode, or something. We're not sure.'

Nobody on the ground was sure what was happening either. Fotheringay's two minutes had long since passed. Tiberius was making groaning noises, and those nearest to it started to feel it heating up. Uneasy, they began to edge further away from the cannon.

'It's quite alright. Obviously, steam is a hot vapour. Perfectly normal. Hastings!' Fotheringay beckoned the man over and hissed: 'What's happening? Didn't I pull that lever all the way down? Go and check, man!' By now, the cannon was starting to glow red, and either steam or smoke was filtering out of the end of the barrel. Hastings hadn't quite reached the gun when it exploded, sending shards of metal flying through the air. Hastings dropped to his knees with a scream, clutching his hand. Blood was seeping through his fingers. Meanwhile, the hose connecting the cannon to the steam pipe had blown free, and it twisted and spun around like an angry snake, emitting searing clouds of steam. Edward had been saying 'Wait…wait…wait', but at the moment he heard the crack of the gun exploding, he shouted 'Now!' and Daniel took the most dramatic photograph of his career. 'Quick! Change the plate, point the camera to the sky and wait for my command.'

'Nearly…nearly…can you see it? Any time now.' Daniel was amazed to find that filling his camera lens was an enormous airship. The doorway to the gondola was open and crammed with several figures. Edward watched Oliver tossing out copies of the 'Rebels' story to the astonished observers. Jake was waving, his metal hand catching the sunlight. Charlotte was smiling, her petticoats fluttering in the breeze, and Billy appeared to be throwing buns at the military chiefs. On the side of the airship, Edward saw the evidence of Jake's handiwork for the first time. The word 'Rebel' was written in large red letters.

Hastings' jaw dropped. Not only was his nemesis, Hooky, cheerfully waving at him, but there too was the harlot he had seen at the park gates. It was all too much for him. He looked at the bright red blood pouring from his wounded finger, and then he fainted. One of the booklets fluttered down from the airship and came to rest on his forehead.

Charlotte disappeared. Edward guessed where she was.

She had gone to take control of the airship. Maybe Cissie had been holding the airship steady but now Charlotte had taken over the controls and the Rebel rose high in the sky and vanished beyond the clouds.

Field Marshal Bellings turned on his heel and silently marched out of the park. A whistle blew, and all the other soldiers fell into line and followed suit. Fotheringay was turning circles in stunned silence. The day was a disaster.

EPILOGUE

'Our first campaign may have had a few hiccups but was ultimately very successful,' said Charlotte, 'What's the new plan?' Everyone looked first at Jake, who shrugged, and then at Oliver.

'Personally, I was planning on having a drink to celebrate,' replied Oliver. Charlotte groaned. 'But that can wait,' he continued, 'First, we have a few errands. Jake has cogs on order to be collected in Bristol, which, given that we came to London from there, should conceal the fact that our final destination is Scotland.'

'I've got lots of ideas for mechanical weapons,' said Jake 'Now that we have shown our hand Oliver and I think they won't just be sending Hastings blundering around the country on a train. We think the Air-Fleet will be tasked with finding us, and we will need more in our armoury than Billy's rock buns.'

'Bloomin' cheek!' replied Billy, 'I 'ad very nearly perfected that recipe!'

'After that, we will travel south to Devon and take young Ruby home.'

'I can't wait to see my family,' said Ruby.

After we've dropped off Ruby, we will head along the south coast and cross to Paris,' explained Oliver, 'I've asked Edward to meet us there. I believe an engineer called Gustave Eiffel is constructing a tower made from wrought iron. I think a photograph of The Rebel tied to it would be splendid. We can toast the airship with a glass of champagne. I'm sure Edward will be able to invent a story about our exploits to accompany it. After Paris, we will head back to the English Channel, and then, travelling through the night, we will stay over the sea and make the journey North to Foula. I can't see anybody managing to track us there.'

'What's that noise,' asked Joshua. 'It sounds like there are pigeons inside the airship!'

'There are. They're wiv me!' replied Billy proudly.

'Are we having pigeon pie?' asked Jake.

'No, we bleedin' ain't!' replied Billy indignantly, 'They're homing pigeons. I got quite pally with the geezer in the bakery dahn The Rookery. Two of 'em are 'is, so they can take a message back to 'im, and e's given me some chicks; then once I've trained 'em up they can be used to carry messages back and forth when we're on Foula. It's not like there's a bleedin' telegraph office there!'

'A brilliant idea. We are developing quite a little network; there's Old Nick and Maggie's brother, Freddy, who are both working at the Steam Works and can keep us informed, not to mention Edward.

Edward was at his new printers, proofreading the latest instalment of the 'Chronicles of The Rebel Runaways.' He was amazed by how successful they had become in such a short time. Two things contributed towards this popularity. Firstly, he was an enigma. No one knew who he was, and that mystery fuelled interest and speculation. Secondly, with his public hat on as the new roving reporter for Reuters, the events he witnessed gave his Chronicles credibility. He had managed to bridge his period of unemployment without his wife getting wind of it. The 'roving' nature of his new job meant that his wife could stay in the country, and he could visit her. He couldn't help regretting that he had a lot more fun when he was in the company of 'The Rebels' than confined to the stultifying atmosphere of the family home. Maybe that issue would be resolved in the future.

Field Marshal Bellings' reputation was damaged, but he clung to power. He hadn't severed connections with Fotheringay because they had several business ideas in the pipeline that would increase his personal fortune. After Reuters had reported the Tiberius debacle, it was initially a national scandal. However, having access to government coffers, Bellings managed to sweeten the press at several exclusive dinners, by hinting that it might be in his remit to award Knighthoods. Bellings was dismayed that he had to reshuffle his cabinet to include members of the Air-Fleet, a military wing that he found devoid of tradition and respectability. However, they had their uses; they had only one mission - to track down and destroy the so-called Rebel Runaways!

Fotheringay couldn't decide whether the financial impact of the failed test, when the government cancelled a contract that would have quadrupled his fortune, hurt more than the disgrace he felt knowing people were laughing at him behind his back. He was constantly instructing decorators to paint over obscene drawings on the factory walls casting aspersions on the effectiveness of his weapon. Strangely, one aspect of the affair he felt little no remorse about was the role of his daughter in all this. Perhaps it would have been different if she had been a boy, he found female company annoying at the best of times, but he felt she was no longer a daughter to him. One thing that Bellings and he shared was a determination to rid the world of all Rebel Runaways!

'Santé! Cheers!' announced Oliver, holding his glass up to peer at the Arc de Triomphe through it. 'A mes amis, Les rebelles en fugue, The Rebel Runaways!'

'Oh, God!' said Charlotte. 'That's his third bottle of champagne. It looks like I'll be steering the airship all the way to Scotland!'

The End

A NOTE FROM THE AUTHOR

I hope you have enjoyed my book and will look out for other titles in the 'Rebel Runaways' series.

I want to thank Rachel Laurence for her input into all my books. As an actress, she does fantastic work narrating the audiobooks, but before that, she plays a crucial part in the editing process.

 I am also the author of the 'Stuck' series from Amazon. They are stand-alone time travel books suitable for adults and children 8+. You can see them by visiting this page on my website: www.stuckdave.co.uk/blink

You can also join my mailing list and find information about upcoming publications and have the opportunity to win free stuff! I would love it if you followed me on Instagram, too: @stuckdavewrites

I would be extremely grateful if you could write a review of my book on Amazon. Even if you didn't buy this book yourself from Amazon, you could still post a review there.

The second book in the series, "Troubled Skies" will be published in November 2023

Troubled Skies

The Rebel Runaways are on one side of the line; Fotheringay and the Government are on the other. No one will give up the fight.

In a tale of two continents, the Rebel Runaways seek to defeat the illegal activities of slave traders secretly funded by the Prime Minister and Fotheringay. Joshua, an ex-slave, has the motivation, Charlotte has the skills to fly the airship and the crew must work together to succeed. Is another cargo of Africans destined for a life of misery? Meanwhile, a Trades Union march in England is organised to protest against cruel working conditions, unaware that the Government and Fotheringay have planned a lethal reception for them.

In a world where injustice rules, can the Rebel Runaways win this struggle?